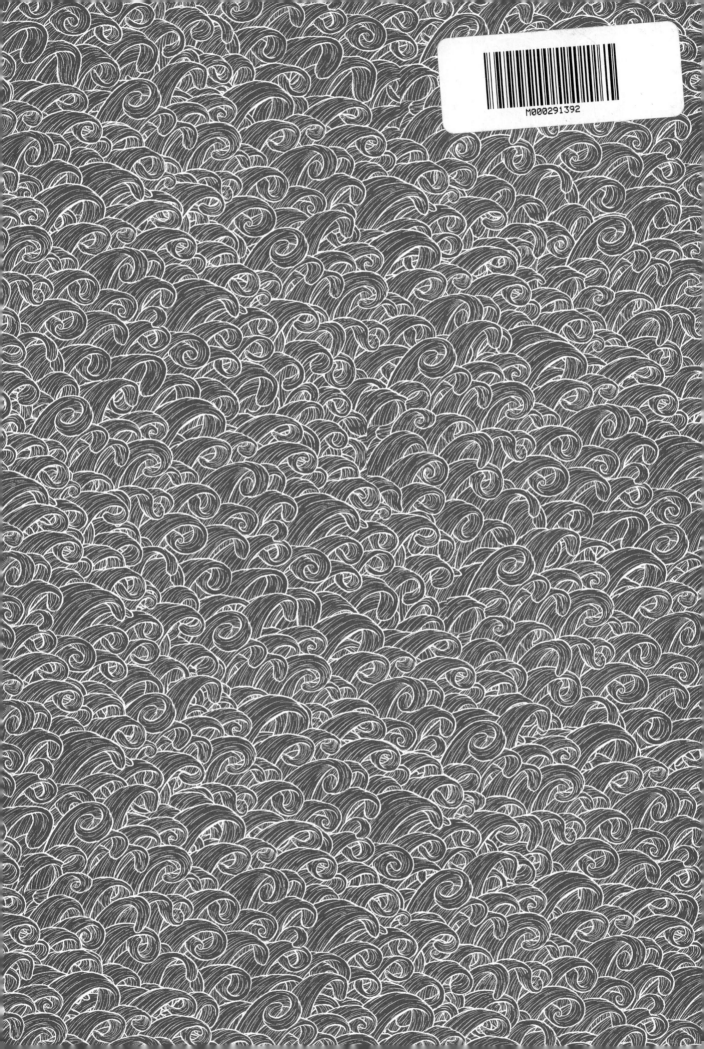

VIKINGS, MONKS, PHILOSOPHERS, WHORES

OLD FORMS, UNEARTHED

Curated by Darren Franich and Graham Weatherly

© 2009 McSweeney's Quarterly Concern and the contributors, San Francisco, California. Every so often, we'll have a meeting here at the McSweeney's HQ, where we ask interns—our heroes and lifeblood—to tell us what they would put in the magazine if they had their druthers. Over the years, the results have been pretty great. Dominic Luxford, an intern a few years ago, wanted poetry in *McSweeney's*, so we asked him to come up with an innovative way to present it. The result was *Poets Picking Poets*, which became a section of Issue 22 and later a standalone paperback book. Not too long after that issue appeared, Darren Franich and Graham Weatherly pitched the idea of an issue celebrating neglected or deceased literary forms, and it immediately intrigued everyone. They went at the idea with a vengeance, and a year later—the research, commissioning, writing, and editing of this issue took a very long time—here we are, with an astonishing array of forms and genres that you've likely never heard of, but which you might very well grow attached to. The pantoum, for example, has already become popular around the office and among our online readers (many of whom sent in their examples of the form). And we expect that the whore dialogue, hilarious and profane and very practical, might catch on again, especially with our readers, many of whom are experts in both cleaning and sexual technique. So we hope you'll enjoy this issue, and that those of you who have recently graduated or been laid off will consider McSweeney's for your internship needs. You will be valued, if not adequately paid. INTERNS & VOLUNTEERS: Juliet Litman, Kathleen Alcott, Jacob Bromberg, Joanna Green, Julia Minkin, Rebecca Nieto, Alex Ludlum, Lindsay Quella, Megan Rickel, Nicholas Koch, Adrienne Mahar, Tess Thackara, Onnesha Roychoudhuri, Cassandra Neyenesch, Christina Rush, Ben Jahn. ALSO HELPING: Alvaro Villanueva, Chris Ying, Michelle Quint, Brian McMullen, Eliana Stein, Greg Larson, Jesse Nathan, Christopher Benz. COPY EDITORS: Oriana Leckert, Caitlin Van Dusen. WEBSITE: Chris Monks. SUPPORT: Darren Franich. OUTREACH: Angela Petrella. CIRCULATION: Heidi Meredith. MANAGING EDITOR: Jordan Bass. PUBLISHER: Eli Horowitz. EDITOR: Dave Eggers.

COVER ILLUSTRATION: Scott Teplin.

THANKS: Carrie Reed, Leo Tak-hung Chan, Bradford K. Mudge, Dominic Luxford, Maddie Oatman, Jessica Johnson, Peter Mack, Candice Chan, John D. Slater, Alix Van Buskirk, Mercedes Berlanga Sánchez, and Priya Reddy.

INTRODUCTION

by DARREN FRANICH *and* GRAHAM WEATHERLY

Everything about the way we write changes constantly. New forms are created and destroyed, conjoined with others and absorbed back into the cultural mainstream; parchment is replaced by pen and paper, which is replaced by predictive text on Finnish cell phones. In the wake of those changes are dozens of dead forms from every corner of civilization, strange and wonderful styles thousands of miles and hundreds of years removed from what we read now. With this issue, we've dug up those old genres, dusted them off, and recruited writers to revitalize the ones we thought demanded it.

Some of the approaches included here flourished in their time; others existed only as brief mutations, freak leaps forward, like fish crawling out of the ocean and then crawling back in. By bringing them together, we aim to offer a haphazard album of where writing has been over the last two millennia. By working with contemporary writers, we're hoping to bring these styles back into our world.

Our genres are, in chronological order: the Socratic dialogue, probably the best known, the one that helped the West illuminate human nature and the workings of the universe; the biji, a popular style in China for over a thousand years, composed of miscellaneous observations, musings, and tall tales; the legendary saga, an Icelandic form that laid the groundwork for modern-day fantasy stories; the consuetudinary, which documented the daily schedule of a monastery to the last spare moment;

the whore dialogue, a conversational progenitor of erotica, filled with exacting anatomic detail; the Graustarkian romance, a sort of adventure story envisioning a country just across the border from the recognizable Western world; and the nivola, our youngest genre, which attempted to push the novel and its characters beyond their notional boundaries. There are also, in here, eight new pantoums and five new senryū, examples of still-kicking poetic forms that aren't as celebrated as they should be. These poems are the result of a call for submissions we put up on the McSweeney's website last spring—we received 473 of them, and even though we could include only a few, it was a thrill to find so many people willing to dive in.

It was just as heartening to see how enthusiastic our other authors were about their genres. After receiving a mountain of printed material devoted to the barely translated form we'd assigned him, Douglas Coupland said "I think I was born to biji." Will Sheff read a few dozen Nordic legends before asking "Any idea on a rough word count? Let me know so I can figure out how many freakin' generations to cram into my epic sweep." (He crammed in several.) David Thomson responded to our pitch with "Just say yes or no to this: Kafka, Woolf, Hemingway, Chaplin, and Sontag are debating the best movie ever made." (We said yes.)

The pieces they sent in made us want to run up and down the stairs as fast as we could. To make sure they come across that way for everyone else, we've included short excerpts from original instances of each form before each piece, and in the margins you'll find other connections and cross-references and echoes. We're hoping those notes will establish a bit of context for what's going on here, but this is not a research text: this is a paean to the weird, beautiful, missing links of literature. If you read this and feel the need to track down an original whore dialogue or a monastery scroll or George Barr McCutcheon's *The Prince of Graustark*, which lacks the gravitas of *Beverly of Graustark* but adds in a layer of farcical meta-satire (it's the *Die Another Day* of the Graustark series), then we've done something right.

In the following pages, you'll find coffeehouse philosophizing, poolside chatter, and road trips gone awry. You'll find kingdoms at war, and a new religion, and the end of the world. There are trains, yachts, horses, and helicopters. There are creatures you didn't know existed and places you won't want to leave. We want to show you what you've been missing—or some of it, at least.

PANTOUM

LIFE SPAN: C. 1400 AD–present; *earlier, in oral form*

NATURAL HABITAT: Malaysia

PRACTITIONERS: Tun Sri Lanang, Munshi Abdullah,
John Ashbery, Carolyn Kizer, Marilyn Hacker

CHARACTERISTICS: Repetitive, trancelike

A Western descendant of the Malay *pantun*, a pantoum is a poem composed in quatrains, in which the second and fourth lines of each stanza reappear (with small alterations) as the first and third lines of the next stanza, and the first and third lines of the first stanza return as the last and second lines, respectively, of the final stanza. There is no set length, rhyme scheme, or subject matter for a pantoum, and artful manipulation of the repeated lines is encouraged.

Pantuns by anonymous writers were part of the Malay oral tradition long before they began to be recorded. (The image above comes from a roughly two-hundred-year-old edition of the Hikayat Hang Tuah, *a collection of Malay legends chronicling the life of a warrior named Hang Tuah, first published in the early seventeenth century. The* Hikayat *contains some of the first known written examples of pantuns.) When French poets rediscovered the form in the nineteenth century, they were drawn to the* pantun berkait—*a pantun form made up of interlocking verses.*

UNTITLED PANTUN BERKAIT

author unknown

—TRANSLATED 1812 AD—

Butterflies sport on the wing around,
They fly to the sea by the reef of rocks
My heart has felt uneasy in my breast,
From former days to the present hour.

They fly to the sea by the reef of rocks.
The vulture wings its flight to Bandan.
From former days to the present hour,
Many youths have I admired.

The vulture wings its flight to Bandan,
Dropping its feathers at Patani.
Many youths have I admired,
But none to compare with my present choice.

His feathers he let fall at Patani.
A score of young pigeons.
No youth can compare with my present choice,
Skilled as he is to touch the heart.

Translated by William Marsden.

CIRCUS

a new pantoum by Jennifer Michael Hecht

My people were existential thugs.
At circus, monkeys in derbies rode us.
Muttering, *Life*, in a full-bodied shrug,
at circus we swept up the sawdust.

At circus, monkeys in derbies rode us,
while the great rode feathered horses.
At circus we swept up the sawdust,
the dove's debris and patrons' losses.

While the great rode feathered horses,
humming to Pegasus, *Oh Peggy Sue*,
we'd unglove, debrief, and pocket losses.
Tanneries are what my people knew.

Brushing Pegasus to strains of "Peggy Sue,"
catching acrobats. Shadow of a big top,
tailor's tales of what the ball gown knew.
Sequins and confetti on a rag mop.

Catch an acrobat's shadow on the big top
muttering, *Life*, with a bruise. Shrugged
sequins; drooped confetti like a rag mop.
My people were existential thugs.

MILLTOWN AUSPICE

a new pantoum by Ben Jahn

How to explain his death—with humor
The best jokes start serious:
He fell asleep on the beach with his pockets full of bread
Seagulls carried him away—

The best jokes start serious:
The Governor went north (the mills full of men) God knows
Seagulls carried him away—
It was a thick-fog day, and still

The Governor went north (the mills full of men) God knows
How to explain his death—with humor
It was a thick-fog day, and still
He fell asleep on the beach with his pockets full of bread

JACK DAVIS

a new pantoum by Tony Trigilio

Jack saw CRY OF BATTLE, VAN HEFLIN, WAR IS HELL
advertised on the Texas Theater marquee
and he figured he'd take in a double feature.
It was an hour after Kennedy was shot.

Under the Texas Theater marquee,
Oswald snuck past the ticket-taker
just as news broke that Kennedy was shot.
A suspicious shoe-store manager saw him.

Oswald snuck past the ticket-taker,
sweating, collar up, cursing his shadow.
A suspicious shoe-store manager saw him
and pointed the police to the picture show.

Sweating, collar up, cursing his shadow,
Oswald walked a far mean streak down the aisle.
The shoe salesman pointed police to *War Is Hell*,
where nearly all the seats were empty.

Oswald walked a far mean streak to Jack's row,
crossed in front of Jack and sat beside him.
With nearly all the seats empty,
He sat down as if the two of them planned it.

He crossed in front of Jack and sat beside him—
then, strangely, moved two seats away.
Oswald sat down, as if he planned it all along,
a conspirator's rendezvous in the dark.

Moving two seats away was, in Jack's opinion,
a signal—a complicated dance
(a conspirator's rendezvous in the dark).
This was some kind of covert contact.

If this was a signal, a complicated dance,
Jack failed it. Oswald got up again—
to make some kind of covert contact
with the man sitting in the row behind him.

Failing, Oswald got up again,
but the police turned on the house lights.
With two men now sitting in the row behind him,
Jack took his popcorn and fled to the lobby.

"Well, it's all over now," Oswald allegedly said,
as the cops shut down the double feature.
They meant to hold the crowd for questioning.
But someone snuck out before *War Is Hell*.

PANTEENTOUM

a new pantoum by Bill Tarlin

I'll kick your ass at State and Madison
Zero to the zero crosshair corner
Prepare to taste my downtown medicine
Feed a meter for the county coroner

Zero to the zero crosshair corner
I draw a bead on your unkempt head
Feed a meter for the county coroner
Or call street sweepers in instead

I draw a bead on your unkempt head
You called me out to stake a claim
Well call street sweepers in instead
You're dust, you're ash, before my flame

You called me out to stake a claim?
Don't think I didn't see her first
You're dust, you're ash, before my flame
She'll wear your nuts hung on her purse

Don't think I didn't see her first
She touched my gun, I met her mom
She'll wear your nuts hung on her purse
and go with me to the senior prom

She touched my gun, I met her mom
Prepare to taste my downtown medicine
Don't talk to me 'bout the senior prom
I'll kick your ass at State and Madison

WHORE DIALOGUE

LIFE SPAN: 1534–1740 AD

NATURAL HABITAT: Italy, France, England

PRACTITIONERS: Pietro Aretino, Abbé du Prat,
    Nicolas Chorier

CHARACTERISTICS: Graphic, erotic, obscene, instructional

The whore dialogue was an early type of erotic writing, combining bawdy, censor-baiting tales of sexuality with an educational veneer. In the dialogues, conversation usuually takes place between a young and sexually inexperienced maid (often a few days away from her wedding night) and an older, crasser married friend, and tends to be divided into "before" and "after" sections: in the first part, the older friend educates the maid, and in the second, the maid relates her newfound knowledge.

A DIALOGUE BETWEEN A MARRIED LADY AND A MAID

a whore dialogue by NICOLAS CHORIER

—1660 AD—

Chorier's dialogue was originally published in France, under the title Aloisiae Sigeae Toletanae Satyra Sotadica de arcanis Amoris et Veneris *("Aloisia Sigea of Toledo's Sotadic Satire about the Secrets of Love and Venus"—Chorier pretended that "Aloisia Sigea of Toledo" was the work's true author). Eighty years later, it caused a scandal in England after an abridged and unauthorized translation was released. The dialogue portrays two women: Octavia, a blushing young lady uncertain what to expect from her marriage to gallant Philander, and Tullia, her older, married cousin.*

OCTAVIA: Teach me exactly every Thing that is fit for me to know; what Sort of Pain it will be, and how long it will last; I had rather have it sharp and short, than have it last, tho' moderate.

TULLIA: That Part of thy Body which is under the Belly, between the Thighs, to which Men give so many Names, but is chiefly called by them C—t, and which is so prettily shaded with Hair, is the Field where *Philander* will begin the Fight; you never yet observed the Make of it, and therefore I will describe it unto thee. Without is a long Slit, and which in Women that are most made for Enjoyment, is high and forward upon the Belly, and not low and backward, as some Women have it, more like Cows than Women.

This Slit is made with two Lips, which being opened gently, discover inward as red as a Cherry, with two other Lips, which are called Wings, or Nymphs; and under them, about a Finger's Breadth, or more within, are in Virgins, as thou art, four little rising Buds, which, joining together and leaving only a little Hole between, stop up the best Part of the Passage into the Womb, and give us all the Trouble Men meet with in deflowering us.

OCTAVIA: I do foresee, that in the Attempt, there will be a great deal of Pain; for I myself can scarce endure to touch them with my Finger.

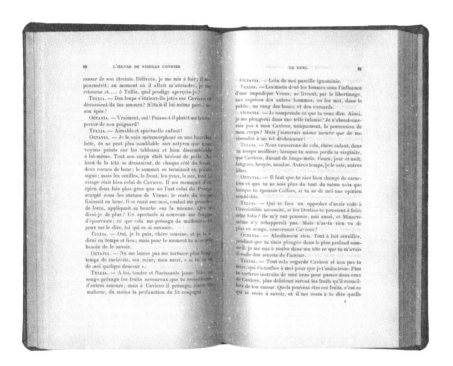

TULLIA: Let me finish my Description. Towards the upper Part of the C—t, is a thing they call *Clitoris*; which is a little like a Man's P——k, for it will swell and stand like his; and being rubbed gently by his Member, will send forth a Liquor, which when it comes away, leaves us in a Trance, as if we were dying, all our Senses being lost, and our Eyes shut, our Hearts languishing on one Side, our Limbs extended, and, in a Word, there follows a dissolving of our whole Person and melting in such inexpressible Joys, as none but those who feel them can express or comprehend…

OCTAVIA: You describe Things so exactly, that methinks I see all that is within me.

TULLIA: Let me see it a little; open your Legs.

OCTAVIA: I do; what do you see now?

TULLIA: Ah! Pretty Creature! How Cherry-red it is!

OCTAVIA: Oh hold, *Tullia*, you tickle me so that I am not able to endure it; take away that wicked Finger, it hurts me.

TULLIA: Well, I pity thee strangely; this pretty Shell, prettier than that out of which Venus herself was born, will be sadly torn by *Philander*. Nay, I begin to be concerned for him too; for the Entrance of this Paradise is so narrow, that it will be with great Difficulty, and no small Pain, e'er that he himself will get admittance. Did you ever see the Thing he has between his Legs?

OCTAVIA: I never saw it, but felt it hard, big and long.

TULLIA: Thy Mother is overjoyed with the Reputation he has of being the best provided young Man in all this City, but it will cost thee some tears; yet be not afraid, my Husband had the same Reputation, and with Reason, and yet I am alive and well.

OCTAVIA: Prithee, let me see how your C—t is, since it had such a Monster within it.

TULLIA: Do, my pretty *Octavia*. Here, I open my Legs a Purpose.

OCTAVIA: Lord! What a Gap is here! I can thrust my whole Hand in almost; how strong it smells! Sure the Roses are all gone here, which you find in mine.

TULLIA: You are very pleasant, but when once you have had a Child, you will be as I am, for this is a necessary Consequence of Marriage.

Image from L'Oeuvre de Nicolas Chorier.

A DIALOGUE BETWEEN TWO MAIDS IN THE TWENTY-FIRST CENTURY, ONE OF WHOM IS SKEEZY

a new whore dialogue by MARY MILLER

I

MARCI: Put that thing down and talk to me. I'm bored.

ASHLEY: Swim some laps.

MARCI: I don't feel like getting wet.

ASHLEY: It looks like Sarah Jessica finally got rid of that weird chin mole. See?

MARCI: Photoshop, I bet. You're not gonna fill me in?

ASHLEY: About the wedding? The flowers cost so much we had to hire my cousin Arthur to take pictures.

MARCI: The short one?

ASHLEY: He'll probably cut the top of everyone's head off.

MARCI: But more importantly: have you let Brian do you yet?

ASHLEY: We're still V-teaming it. We signed a pledge. I want to say fuck it but he's being strong. It's so annoying.

This kind of friendly goading is common in whore dialogues—often, the more experienced speaker will begin by coaxing the other woman into the discussion. From Chorier's *A Dialogue Between a Married Lady and a Maid*:

TULLIA: Did you feel nothing else but his Finger?
OCTAVIA: I did; But what an Impudence is mine, to relate that which remains!
TULLIA: Prithee, as if I had not felt the same Thing before. Go on.

MARCI: That's completely annoying.

ASHLEY: If I didn't want to do it so bad he'd be begging me for it.

MARCI: Of course he would. Men are so weak.

ASHLEY: He barely even touches me. He says if he gets to a certain point he can't stop, like the Incredible Hulk. There's no turning back.

MARCI: Did you see that movie?

ASHLEY: I love Liv Tyler. She's *so* pretty.

MARCI: I hate how soft her voice is, though. She's too tall to have a voice like that. She's not, like, Natalie Portman.

ASHLEY: Is it true that vibrators are still illegal? Lauren told me they're against the law. If that's true then that's the biggest load of bullhonky I've ever heard.

Many early whore dialogues, first written in France, Spain, and Italy, came into English by way of pirated editions. They were often sold under altered or entirely new titles, with no mention of the original publishing house or author.

MARCI: They sell them behind the counters. You have to go downtown, by the soup kitchen. I forget the name. It looks pervy because there're bars on all the windows and hoopties parked out front but a bunch of lesbians work there.

ASHLEY: Oh my gah.

MARCI: You mean God.

ASHLEY: I don't say "God." I say gah.

MARCI: Oh my God oh my God oh my God.

As risqué as the whore dialogues were, some of them shared this avoidance of outright blasphemy. In *Venus in the Cloister*, by "the Abbé du Prat" (a pen name) the two promiscuous nuns often say "Ah, Lard!" to each other. The dialogue nevertheless earned its publisher England's first obscenity conviction.

ASHLEY: Have you noticed how many girls who look like lesbians like the Penis?

MARCI: I think everyone likes the Penis. Lesbians just don't like how men are attached to the Penis.

ASHLEY: I bet you're right.

MARCI: I have, like, four college friends who are lesbians. And two of them were born that way.

ASHLEY: That's cool.

MARCI: I wonder if you still have your hymen.

ASHLEY: I hate that word! Don't say it or I'll freak out. I'm not kidding.

MARCI: Do you use tampons?

ASHLEY: Of course I use tampons. What do you think I use?

MARCI: I don't know. Sometimes I call you to go to the country club and you say you have an earache.

ASHLEY: I have narrow ear canals. Besides, I have a pool right here. What do I need to go to the country club for?

MARCI: I know you don't play sports.

ASHLEY: What do sports have to do with anything?

MARCI: Have you ever been fingered?

ASHLEY: A couple of times. They didn't know what they were doing.

MARCI: I bet you've still got it. I bet you'll, like, bleed in the shape of Africa and Brian'll hang your bedsheet over the balcony for everyone to see.

ASHLEY: Knowing me I'll probably bleed in the shape of Chile.

MARCI: That would be horrible.

ASHLEY: Or Italy.

MARCI: Shut up.

ASHLEY: We should go downtown and buy me a vibrator right now.

MARCI: It's Sunday. I'll get you a Rabbit for your bachelorette party. The Rabbit is amazing. It has bunny ears for clit stimulation.

ASHLEY: When I was little I had a ton of rabbits.

MARCI: But then your dad made you get rid of all but one and you cried for a week.

ASHLEY: I can't believe you remember that.

MARCI: I also remember when you cried at camp because you were homesick, and then your period started.

ASHLEY: I hated camp.

Whore dialogues emphasized the trauma of a virgin's first time as much as they did the pleasure of it. From *A Dialogue Between a Married Lady and a Maid*:

He put his Finger into the Slit, which is a very little one, and he could hardly get it in, because I felt some little Pain; but at the same Time he cried out, Oh I have a Maid! A Virgin to my Share! And immediately opening my Legs with Force, he threw himself between them flat upon his Face.

Both glass dildos and masturbating nuns make several appearances in the original dialogues. *Venus in the Cloister* shows them together, the latter making use of the former:

> He shewed me a certain *Instrument of Glass*, which he had of her I have been telling you of; and he assured me, that she told him there were above fifty of them in their House, and that every one, from the *Abbess* down to the last *Profest* handled *them* oftener than their *Beads*.

In Michel Millot's *The School of Venus*, the nuns are less well-equipped:

> Wenches that are not rich enough to buy statues must content themselves with dildoes made of Velvet, or blown in glass, Prick fashion, which they fill with lukewarm milk, and tickle themselves therewith, as with a true Prick, squirting the milk up into their bodies when they are ready to spend. Some mechanick Jades frig themselves with candles of about four in the pound; Others as most Nuns do make use of their fingers.

MARCI: You don't need a vibrator, you know. You can just use your hands.

ASHLEY: That sounds messy.

MARCI: Ashley. Come on. Tell me you've masturbated before.

ASHLEY: Nuh-uh. How do you do it?

MARCI: What do you mean, "How do you do it?" You get naked and touch yourself. David has pornos I watch sometimes. He keeps them in his safe with his pot.

ASHLEY: I don't know…

MARCI: My favorite one is of this really hot girl riding a carousel horse. This guy eats her out for like twenty minutes and she's on the horse the whole time. I swear she actually comes, too.

ASHLEY: I think I'll just make something up in my head, like I'm a cocktail waitress at a strip club.

MARCI: And you decide to prostitute yourself for extra money?

ASHLEY: Something like that.

MARCI: That's a pretty good one.

ASHLEY: Did I tell you we're going to Aruba for our honeymoon? They have these weird-looking trees called divi-divis and the native language is Papiamento. Papiamento!

MARCI: Does Brian have a big dick?

ASHLEY: It's not huge or anything.

MARCI: How big is it?

ASHLEY: I don't know. I've only seen one besides his and it was tiny. I remember being like, *What is that little thing supposed to do?*

MARCI: He'll probably just stay up all night playing blackjack at the casino.

ASHLEY: He better stay up all night fucking me.

MARCI: I think he has a gambling problem.

ASHLEY: He does not. There's going to be a lot of recreational fucking at our house. A ton of it.

MARCI: Small dicks are disappointing but there's an upside: it'll be easier for him to fuck you in the ass.

ASHLEY: I don't want to be fucked in the ass.

Most protagonists in the whore dialogues shared this attitude. Anal sex is almost entirely absent from the genre.

MARCI: You don't know until you try. Your asshole has about a billion nerve endings. The only bad thing is that once you start he'll want it every time. You shouldn't start. I take that back. Don't start.

ASHLEY: Stop trying to freak me out with all this ass-fucking.

MARCI: I'm sorry. I'm going to flip over now. My boobs are getting burnt.

ASHLEY: I'd like to have some straight missionary position first.

MARCI: I love it. You've got to lube that thing up, though. Don't try it without a shitload of lube.

ASHLEY: Could you stop talking about this? I'm getting turned on and it's grossing me out.

MARCI: Sorry. I won't say another word about it. Do you have any popsicles?

ASHLEY: I think we have Fudgsicles? They're like a hundred calories and they're amazing.

Describing her first time in *The School of Venus*, Katy says,

> There is not that sweetmeat or variety whatsoever, that is so pleasant to the Palate as spending is to a Cunt, it tickleth us all over, and leave us half dead.

II

MARCI: Did you use the Rabbit yet?

ASHLEY: Yeah.

MARCI: And?

ASHLEY: I liked it.

When Tullia, in *A Dialogue...*, sleeps with her husband for the second time, she experiences

MARCI: You *liked* it?

ASHLEY: Okay, it's incredible. I'm like, addicted.

> a sweet Tickling, and at the End, a Seizure in every Joint and Limb, which made me languishing lay my Head on one Side, and in Sighs and Short Breathing, express the inconceivable Pleasure of all my Senses.

MARCI: You won't get addicted.

ASHLEY: I think my mom knows when I'm using it, though. I'll turn it on and all of a sudden she wants to know if pizza's okay for dinner. Of course pizza's okay for dinner.

MARCI: I never liked to masturbate at my parents' house, either. It was like I could feel my dead grandmothers watching me or something.

ASHLEY: It's like all the old people who've ever died are elbowing each other.

MARCI: How'd the stripper fantasy work?

ASHLEY: Cocktail waitress.

MARCI: You should just let yourself be the stripper. It's a fantasy, for fuck's sake. Be the stripper.

ASHLEY: I kind of like being the cocktail waitress. It's less obvious.

MARCI: *It's a strip-club fantasy.* It's like the most obvious fantasy in history.

ASHLEY: When I was the waitress all the managers wanted to fuck me.

MARCI: Of course they did. You were new.

ASHLEY: But I resisted.

MARCI: But then you broke down and let them gang-bang you.

ASHLEY: No. Yes. Brian loves it, too. He's all like, go get your Rabbit!

MARCI: Boys usually don't mind the help.

ASHLEY: He says he wants to please me.

MARCI: Of course he wants to please you. Only total dicks don't want to please you. Just don't feel like you have to go overboard for him. I think it's best to be as incompetent as possible, at least at first. Serve him bloody chicken and wash all his underwear with a red T-shirt and if he gets mad, cry.

ASHLEY: I can cry at the drop of a hat.

MARCI: You have to tell yourself they owe it to you. One time I had this boyfriend who made me vegetarian lasagna from scratch while

Venus in the Cloister begins with an older, more experienced nun catching a younger one in the act of masturbation:

Dost thou not know, my little Fool, what it was I could see? Why I saw thee in an action, in which I will serve thee myself, if thou wilt, and in which my Hand shall now perform that Office which thine did just now so charitably…

Octavia, in *A Dialogue…*, attempts to conceal her pleasure from Philander at first ("blushing and hiding my face, I said that if he felt any Moisture, it was that which he had put into me, and not any that I had sent out"), but he tells her,

Most Women are in that Error that they think they ought to hide their Joys from us, but it is the greatest Mistake in the World, for our Pleasures consist more in theirs, than our own… none but Brutes can be delighted only with that unusual Evacuation of easing themselves.

he was shaking so bad from the DTs I thought he'd die on my kitchen floor.

ASHLEY: Which one was that?

MARCI: Gary Boone.

ASHLEY: He had a caveman forehead.

MARCI: Yeah, but he'd go get me Krystal's at two o'clock in the morning and he'd eat my pussy for hours. Even when I'd just been jogging, he'd be like, let me at it.

ASHLEY: That's so gross.

MARCI: I should have kept him, probably.

III

MARCI: Do you like my new bikini?

ASHLEY: It's cute. I like the flag theme.

MARCI: Shut up. Merikelly helped me pick it out. She said it made my boobs look giant.

ASHLEY: Your boobs *are* giant. With boobs like that you're supposed to be camouflaging them. Don't you read *Lucky?*

MARCI: I only read *O.*

ASHLEY: You're kidding.

MARCI: Dead serious.

ASHLEY: So. Aren't you going to ask me?

MARCI: We were discussing my boobs first, how good they look.

ASHLEY: They're amazing.

MARCI: Thanks.

ASHLEY: I'm sort of mad at you.

MARCI: How come?

ASHLEY: You didn't wear your dress at the reception.

Compared to the number of ways the vagina is described and assessed in the whore dialogues, little mention is made of breasts, or of breast size. Penis size is, however, considered very important. In *Venus in the Cloister*, a nun commenting on a monk at the convent (and punning somewhat on the color of his habit) says, "He is well made and a beautiful young Fellow. For my part, I call him nothing else but my *large white Thing*."

MARCI: I know. I'm sorry. It was too tight. I left it on for a while but then I wanted to sit down and stuff myself with shrimp. Are you mad?

ASHLEY: Well.

MARCI: And it was peach. I don't look good in peach.

ASHLEY: I know. It's okay. My mother was driving me insane. She kept following me around calling me *Sadie, Sadie, Married Lady.*

MARCI: I remember that.

ASHLEY: How drunk was I?

MARCI: You didn't seem that drunk. You were just sort of loud.

ASHLEY: I remember thinking to myself: *You're screaming. You have got to stop screaming.*

MARCI: The food was really good. I liked those little crabcake sandwiches.

ASHLEY: Me too. You know at the hotel he didn't even let me take my dress off? I was nervous because it cost, like, four thousand dollars. He got come on it, of course.

MARCI: Ugh.

ASHLEY: I think he wanted to get come on it, to mark me for life or something.

MARCI: I bet he lasted… three minutes.

ASHLEY: I don't know. Maybe. No, wait—that's a hundred and eighty seconds. It couldn't have taken that long.

MARCI: Too bad.

ASHLEY: Worse was the next morning we had to get up at eight to catch the plane and I was still completely hammered. We almost missed our flight.

MARCI: I love airports but I hate flying.

ASHLEY: Me too.

MARCI: That recirculated air makes me sick.

Mothers tend to be humorously intrusive figures in the genre. In *A Dialogue…*, Tullia's first postcoital moment is interrupted:

> He embraced me still harder, and thrusting his Member up as high as it would go, after two or three more Motions, die'd in my Arms, with infinite Pleasure, just as I had made an End of mine… *Horatio* was about to put in with some roguish Compliment, when he found himself seized by another Hand and kissed as earnestly; it was my Mother, who gave him a thousand Thanks, for having behaved himself so bravely. Thy Victory, said she, was made known to me by *Tullia*'s Cries, but I make no Question, they will hence forward be turned into kind Expressions between you for ever. I was so ashamed to hear my Mother's Voice so near, that I endeavoured to cover Horatio (who was almost naked) with the Bed-Cloaths, and turn myself under 'em…

Octavia has a similar experience.

The first time, in a whore dialogue, is generally not glamorous or romantic. From *The School of Venus:*

KATY: The more he rubbed the more it tickled me, that at last, my hands on which I leaned failed me, and I fell flat on my face.
FRANK: I suppose you caught no harm by the fall.
KATY: None, but he and I dying with pleasure, fell in a Trance, he only having time to say, there have you lost your Maiden-head, my fool.
FRANK: How was it with you? I hope you spent as well as he.

ASHLEY: He gave me the window seat but made me promise he could have it on the way back.

MARCI: What does he need the window seat for?

ASHLEY: I have no idea. When we finally got to the resort, though, this little chimichanga is finishing up our room and she gives Brian these big eyes and he does a double take and then he leaves her these enormous tips every day. Since when does he tip the cleaning lady? She didn't even clean that good. There was like this little nest of hair in the bathroom. Every day I'd look to see if she'd picked it up but she never did.

MARCI: That's gross.

ASHLEY: And the trees are all weird-looking because the wind is *insane*. I'm not kidding. I had to wear a hat every time we left the room.

MARCI: What else did y'all do? Did Brian gamble his cojones off?

ASHLEY: We only went to the casino once. He won fifty dollars so he bought me an Aruba tank top and some other crap.

MARCI: That was sweet.

ASHLEY: I know. He's a sweetie pie. One day we rented a Jeep and drove to this beach called Baby Beach. The sand was so soft and the water was so pretty and shallow.

MARCI: Did the sex get any better?

ASHLEY: A little. He says it'll take practice.

MARCI: Yeah, sometimes it takes practice.

ASHLEY: One night I cried and he cried and we said maybe we shouldn't have gotten married but things improved after that. I think we just needed to put that out there.

MARCI: That's sad.

ASHLEY: It's not sad. It's scary getting married.

MARCI: I'm never getting married.

The sexual politics of the whore dialogues mix together voyeuristic misogyny with proto-feminist female empowerment. In *The School of Venus*, the elder cousin ("Frank") explains why some men prefer less-experienced partners:

KATY: I have but one question more to ask you, who are the most proper for love Concerns, Married Women or Maids?

FRANK: Married Women without question, for they are deeper learned, and have had longer experience in it, knowing all the intrigues of that passion perfectly well.

KATY: Why then do some Men love Maids better?

FRANK: Because they take pleasure to instruct the ignorant, who are more obedient and tractable unto them, letting them do what they please, besides, their Cunts are not so wide but fit their Pricks better, and consequently tickleth them abundantly more.

Octavia's mother, in *A Dialogue…*, who goes in and out of the newly-weds' bedroom before, during, and after their first time together, tells her daughter afterward,

thou art now born to a new Life; and this Night will make an End of shewing you that which the Light of a thousand Days would never do without thy dear *Philander*. Thy Wit and Understanding will clear up with thy Enjoyments, for that very Engine that opens our Bodies, will do the same to our Minds; and make us despise all childish Sports and Amusements, to give our Hearts up to this one heavenly Pleasure, the greatest of all Mortal Delights.

For all its celebration of sex, the whore dialogue often looks toward parenthood with the same excitement. In *The School of Venus*, Katy tells her cousin,

> This I am sure of, it cannot but be a great satisfaction to a Woman, that she hath brought a Rational and living creature into the World, and that one whom she dearly loves had his share in getting it.

ASHLEY: Oh, please, don't kid yourself. I want to have babies already. Your eggs start to dry up at thirty, you know.

MARCI: I'm pretty sure it's thirty-five.

ASHLEY: Either way it's pushing it. And I want three babies: boy, girl, boy.

MARCI: It doesn't work that way.

ASHLEY: I know, but it's like a fifty-fifty chance.

MARCI: Actually, it's a fifty-fifty chance each time so that's like, I don't know what it is but it's not fifty-fifty.

ASHLEY: That's just what I want. I'm not saying I'll get it. But look at my diamond, how sparkly. It's called *marquis cut* and it's over three carats.

MARCI: And football-shaped. That's nice.

LEGENDARY SAGA

LIFE SPAN: mid-1200s–1400 AD; earlier, in oral form

NATURAL HABITAT: Iceland

PRACTITIONERS: Icelandic storytellers

CHARACTERISTICS: Warfare, bloodshed, vengeance passed down
through generations, occasional poetic verse

Written from a vantage point several hundred years removed, legendary
sagas chronicled the conquests of famous Scandinavian adventurers of the
tenth century and earlier, mixing in mythological elements and cosmic
hyperbole with meticulous descriptions of genealogy and conflict. The
protagonists lust for fame and glory, often at the expense of their own
lives; once they've fallen, their battles are taken up by their sons. Luck,
much admired, inevitably runs out.

AN EXCERPT FROM

THE TALE OF RAGNAR'S SONS

a legendary saga

—FIRST KNOWN RECORDING C. 1310 AD—

Like many of the great sagas, The Tale of Ragnar's Sons *(or* Ragnarssona þáttr, Þáttr af Ragnars sonum) *is based on an actual historical figure: Ragnar Lodbrok (also known as "Ragnar Lothrocus," or "Ragnar Hairy Britches"). Composed sometime in the thirteenth century, and collected in Haukr Erlendsson's* Hauksbók *("The book of Haukr") between 1306 and 1310, Ragnar's story includes a number of motifs central to the genre: vengeful children, self-sacrifice, and swordsmen practicing a memorable attack called the blood eagle.*

A T THAT TIME, there was a king called Ella ruling over Northumbria in England. And when he learns that raiders have come to his kingdom, he musters a mighty force and marches against Ragnar with an overwhelming host, and hard and terrible battle ensues. King Ragnar was clad in the silken jacket Aslaug had given him at their parting. But as the defending army was so big that nothing could withstand them, so almost all his men were killed, but he himself charged four times through the ranks of King Ella, and iron just glanced off his silk shirt. Finally he was taken captive and put in a snake-pit, but the snakes wouldn't come near him. King Ella had seen during the day, as they fought, that iron didn't bite him, and now the snakes won't harm him. So he had him stripped of his clothes, and at once snakes were hanging off him on all sides, and he left his life there with much courage.

And when the sons of King Ragnar hear this news, they head west to England and fight with King Ella. But since Ivar wouldn't fight, nor his men, and moreover the English army was immense, they were defeated and fled to their ships and home to Denmark, leaving it at that.

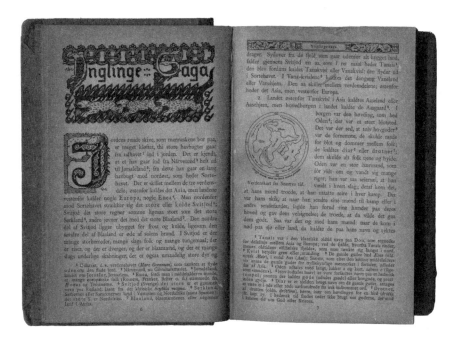

But Ivar stayed in England and went to see King Ella and asked to be compensated for his father. And because King Ella had seen that Ivar didn't want to fight alongside his brothers, he took this for a genuine offer of peace. Ivar asked the king to give him in compensation as much land as he could cover with the biggest old bull-hide he could find, because, he says, he can't very well go home in peace to his brothers if he doesn't get anything. This all seemed aboveboard to Ella and they agree to these terms. Ivar now takes a fresh supple bull-skin and has it stretched out as thin as can be. And then he has the hide sliced into the finest string. Then he has it pulled around a flat stretch of land and marked out foundations. He builds strong city walls, and that town is now called York.

Then Ivar sends word to his brothers and says it's more likely they'll be able to avenge their father now if they come with an army to England. And as soon as Ivar learns they're on their way, he goes to King Ella and says that he doesn't want to keep such news a secret, but he can't really fight against his own brothers; nevertheless he'll go and talk to them and try to make peace. The king agrees. Ivar goes to meet his brothers and incites them to avenge their father, and then goes back to King Ella and says that they're so savage and crazed with fury that they want to fight no matter what. As far as the king can see, Ivar is acting with the utmost faith. Now Ella goes against the brothers with his army.

But when they clash, a good many leaders leave the king and go over to Ivar. The king was outnumbered then, so that the greater part of his forces fell, but he himself was taken captive. Ivar and the brothers now recall how their father was tortured. They now had the eagle cut in Ella's back, then all his ribs severed from the backbone with a sword, so that his lungs were pulled out.

After this battle, Ivar made himself king over that part of England which his forebears had owned before him. He had two brothers born out of wedlock, one called Yngvar, the other Husto. They tortured King Edmund the Saint on Ivar's orders, and then they took his kingdom.

The sons of Lodbrok went raiding in many lands: England, Wales, France, and out over Lombardy. And one time they thought of going to Rome and taking that. And their warrings have become the most famous in all the northlands where Norse is spoken. And when they come back to their realm in Denmark, they shared out the lands between them. Bjorn Ironside got Uppsala and central Sweden and all the lands that belong to that, and it's told that Sigurd Snake-in-Eye had Zealand and Skåne and Halland, and Oslo Fjord.

Sigurd Snake-in-Eye married Blaeja, the daughter of King Ella. Their son was Knut, who was called Horda-Knut, who succeeded his father in Zealand, Skåne and Halland, but Oslo Fjord broke away from his rule. Gorm was his son. He was named after his foster father, the son of Knut the Foundling. He governed all the lands of Ragnar's sons while they were away at war. Gorm Knutsson was the biggest of men and the strongest and the most impressive in every respect, but he wasn't as wise as his forebears had been.

Translated by Peter Tunstall. Image from Snorre Sturlason's Kongesagaer.

BLACK METAL CIRCLE SAGA

a new legendary saga by WILL SHEFF

Øystein Aarseth—better known as Euronymous, a guitarist in the Norwegian black-metal band Mayhem—perished on August 10, 1993, from twenty-three stab wounds to his back and neck. Police quickly arrested Varg Qisling Larssøn Vikernes, who performed under the name Count Grishnackh in the rival black-metal band Burzum. The high-profile murder, along with a spate of church burnings in Norway, helped bolster record sales by both bands and launched the so-called black-metal scene on its path to international infamy.

—OC Weekly, April 24, 2003

I

VIKINGLIGR VELDI

THERE WAS A KING called Gullinguð Four-Sticks, the son of Steina, who reigned over the kingdom of Vingulmörk. Gullinguð was married to Járnkarl, the daughter of a king named Góinn, and their sons were called Blóðlauss and Blóðstjarna. One afternoon as the two boys were fishing, Blóðstjarna grew jealous of how many more fish his brother had caught, and struck him in the head with an oar. The blow dented Blóðlauss's skull and he fell to the bottom of the river and drowned.

When he saw that he had killed his brother, Blóðstjarna ran into the forest and lived there for several years, seeing and talking to no one and eating wild birds and animals, until his hair grew long and his voice became a growl and he didn't know if he was a man or a beast. But after

Sagas often begin with a listing of the key characters, who are usually members of one noble family. *The Saga of Illugi, the Foster Son of Grid* opens with

> There was a king named Hring who ruled in Denmark. He was the son of Skjold Dagsson. This Skjold fought against Herman, as it says in their saga. King Hring had a queen named Sigrid. She was the daughter of Vilhjalm, king of Gaul. They had a son named Sigurd. He was the most handsome of all men and best equipped for great achievements; cheerful with his friends, liberal with wealth, but fierce to his foes.

Retreat to the forest after a particularly shameful deed is a frequent occurrence in the sagas. There, the disgraced usually lingers in solitude until the promise of redemption draws him out. From *The Saga of Hervor and King Heidrek the Wise*, another saga in which fratricide features prominently:

Hofund held a funeral feast for his son, and all grieved at Angantyr's death. Heidrek regretted his deed and lived long in the woods shooting beasts and birds for his food. But when he pondered his case, it occurred to him that if he was never seen again, then nothing good would ever be said of him. It came into his head that he could still be a famous man with great deeds to his name like those of his forebears. He went home.

Vingulmörk is the region of Scandinavia in which modern-day Oslo is located.

Dialogue in the sagas often takes the form of verse. In *The Saga of Ketil Trout*, Gusir says:

Go now into
the bitter sword-clash,
hold your shield before you,
I will shoot hard,
I will turn you into raw meat.

some years had passed and Blóðlauss's body had been carried out to sea, Blóðstjarna said to himself, "If I stay in the forest, all anyone will say of me is that I killed my brother, the greater of my father's sons." He resolved to go back to his father's hall in Vingulmörk.

When he returned, Gullinguð would not see him. But Járnkarl convinced the king to let Blóðstjarna guard over their tributary lands in Skíringssalr, and Blóðstjarna reigned there as an under-king for many years, acquiring a reputation as a wise arbiter in disputes, though everyone called him Blóðstjarna Venomous. When Gullinguð fell in a battle with Leifrvíg, a Swedish king, Blóðstjarna avenged his death and then took his crown. He married a maiden named Skuld, and they had two sons, Eirð and Forfaðir. It's said that they were both strong and hearty young boys and that Forfaðir, with his long blond hair, most resembled his dead uncle Blóðlauss.

II

BLOOD ON ICE

It is now to be told that, after some years had gone by, a creature came to Vingulmörk and began devouring the cattle there. No one had seen any beast that resembled it, and it was considered an unusual thing and a blight on the kingdom. Several of Blóðstjarna's champions tried to attack this creature but returned filled with fear, saying that its hide was so tough no sword could bite it. The creature wandered around Blóðstjarna's kingdom, killing cattle and men as it pleased, and then it disappeared. It returned one year later, and again Blóðstjarna's champions tried to kill it and none could, and again it disappeared and returned a year later, and did this for three years.

In the year that Blóðstjarna's son Forfaðir turned fifteen, it happened that he was walking in the forests on the western side of Víkin just after sunset when he saw a flickering light between the tree trunks. Approaching, Forfaðir saw an old man sitting by a fire, a wide hat covering his face. Forfaðir felt afraid, but the old man asked the boy to approach, speaking this verse:

> You find me at this fire, Forfaðir, waiting for you.
> I've walked a long way, from where there's no time or space.
> A vast green valley—very soon you'll travel there.
> For you I have a fine gift, and foresee greatness.

Forfaðir could see that the old man had only one eye. Before he could say a word, the old man uttered a second verse:

I see you on a stallion, snow-bright, arrow-swift.

I see a slashing sword, steel, fire-forged

Slicing sinew and bone, sealing victory always.

You will father a family, future legends all.

When he had finished speaking, the old man rose and pulled a branch off the ash tree above him, thrusting it into the fire. The branch caught flame and the old man gave it to Forfaðir, pointing him to the mouth of an icy cave in the side of a hill behind them.

Forfaðir trembled with fear, but he walked into the cave, lighting up the walls with the burning branch he'd been given. Inside, after some minutes, he found a long wooden box. He opened it and, within, wrapped in bearskins, saw a sword glinting. When Forfaðir took hold of the sword, all fear left him. When he came out from the cave, the old man had gone and the fire was dead.

Forfaðir called this blade Svartmálmr, and it was said that it could hew through any armor no matter how strong, and that its bearer was always assured of victory. When the creature that had been plaguing Vingulmörk returned, Forfaðir went to it alone with the sword Svart-málmr, puncturing its tough hide until it streamed blood and hacking off both of the creature's heads to bring as gifts to his father. The heads were preserved in large jars of salt.

Word spread that Forfaðir had no fear of man or beast, and everyone called him Forfaðir Hammerheart.

III

EURYNOMOS

Some time passed and Forfaðir's brother Eirð left the kingdom of Vingulmörk. He explored as far as the Dumb Sea, and then went on to settle in Kaupmannahöfn, in Denmark. In time he became king there, and he is out of the saga. Forfaðir, meanwhile, married a woman from the nearby kingdom of Hringaríki; Silfrvængr was her name. Their son, Eysteinn, was born on a morning in early winter, and the saga says that Forfaðir took his son when he was first born and walked outside where for the first time the light struck Eysteinn, and Forfaðir held the child up to the sky and then gently swayed him over the flames of a small fire before cleaning him in the first snow that had fallen on the ground. Eysteinn was a very beautiful child and his parents knew when they looked at his eyes that he would outshine all other men.

Svartmálmr is Old Norse for "Black Metal." Magical weapons like this one are a fixture in the sagas. In *The Saga of Hervor and King Heidrek the Wise*, Sigrlami receives a sword from a pair of dwarves:

> Sigrlami kept that sword and called it Tyrfing. It was the sharpest of swords, and each time it was drawn a light shone from it like a sunbeam. Never could it be bared without killing a man, and with warm blood it would always be sheathed. And nothing, not human nor animal, could live a day if they got a wound from it, no matter how great or small. It never failed to strike, nor did it stop till it hit the earth, and any man who bore it in battle would have victory if he used it.

The Dumb Sea, named for King Dumb, was another name for the Arctic Ocean. King Dumb is a character in the folktale "Bard the Snow-Fell God," a *landvættasogur* (a fictional saga of a land's guardian spirits).

The "adoption" of foster children was a common practice among the ruling class in the centuries in which the sagas are set. It was seen as a way to strengthen political alliances, and to provide insurance for them.

When Eysteinn grew to be nine years old, Forfaðir's old friend and ally, whose name was Sjómaðr, sent his son Vargrækr over for fosterage, as was the custom in those days, and the two lived together in the same chamber. Vargrækr was a lively child, quick-witted and full of schemes and plans. Forfaðir loved them both and the two did everything together, always riding side by side and even dressing and talking alike, until people began to think of them as brothers in blood. At night Forfaðir would sing songs and tell the children tales about his travels, about his slaying the creature that had plagued the kingdom, and about the valley where time and space do not obtain.

One morning, when Forfaðir was out hunting with the two boys, an old man dressed in a cloak and a wide-brimmed hat came into the court at Vingulmörk. He met Blóðstjarna there, and asked to speak with his son, telling Blóðstjarna he had gifts to offer. Blóðstjarna didn't know the old man, who had one eye only, and thought he was a beggar. The old man took great offense, but he offered his gifts again, and asked again to speak with Forfaðir Hammerheart. But Blóðstjarna told him, "What gifts would my son accept from an old blind beggar?" and turned him away. Blóðstjarna didn't tell Forfaðir about his encounter with the old man, and time passed as before.

IV

WAR PIGS

It is now to be told that there was a man called Hjassi who was the son of Leifrvíg from Áttundaland, whom Blóðstjarna had slain some years before. It happened that Hjassi gathered a great host of warriors and marched on Vingulmörk to avenge his father. Blóðstjarna and Forfaðir saw them coming, and they gathered their own army and met Hjassi in battle. Father and son fought side by side, and for a while it seemed as though their small army might be able to overwhelm Hjassi's, but then suddenly Forfaðir notices a great boar, larger than any he's ever seen, fighting alongside Hjassi's army. The boar attacks Blóðstjarna and Forfaðir's warriors, flinging them into the air and battering them to pieces. Forfaðir then says to Blóðstjarna, "The favor that I once saw has now gone against me. This is bad for us, and I think we will die here." Blóðstjarna and Forfaðir fight bravely, but without Forfaðir's former luck Hjassi's army is too great for them, and both men fall there, along with their warriors and their whole court.

Forfaðir's wife Silfrvængr, though, had taken the children Eysteinn

Áttundaland was a region in what is now the Swedish province of Stockholm. Its name translates as "Land of the Eight Hundreds." The "hundred," or *hundare*, was a geographic measurement used to divide territory at the time.

The shift from past tense to present is a quintessential trait of the sagas; usually, it occurs when the storyteller is recounting a pivotal event.

and Vargrækr when she spied Hjassi's men in the distance, and sent them to Forfaðir's ally Sjómaðr with the sword Svartmálmr. Hjassi took Vingulmörk for himself and slaughtered all who were faithful to Blóðstjarna, including Silfrvængr. In some men he cut the Blood Eagle, slicing their ribs from their spine and pulling their lungs out behind them so that they died. But he couldn't find Forfaðir's son, though he looked for him throughout Vingulmörk.

v

INNOCENCE AND WRATH

Eysteinn and Vargrækr grew up together at Sjómaðr's great hall in Björgyn. The two foster brothers trained as fighters, eating and drinking with Sjómaðr's champions and fighting alongside them and growing skilled and powerful through many battles and skirmishes.

When Vargrækr reached his nineteenth year, he was very eager to march to Vingulmörk with Eysteinn to kill Hjassi and avenge the deaths of Blóðstjarna and his foster father Forfaðir. He told this plan to Álfr, the greatest hero of Sjómaðr's court, and Álfr replied, "I had a dream last night that we lived not in this court but in a distant time, and you and I and Eysteinn were marching in the rocky fields of Horðaland, armored in an old-fashioned manner and bearing in front of us the standard of Forfaðir Hammerheart. As we walked, the standard began to bulge and swell in size and our armor grew heavier around our arms and legs and our helms grew in size and covered our eyes until we were as little boys in great suits of armor and we could no longer walk forward even one step. And the standard grew so heavy that it slipped from our hands and tumbled onto the rocks and burst, and entrails and black blood issued from it. I believe this dream means that to march on Hjassi's kingdom at this time will bring about grievous consequences for us."

Álfr's mother had been an elf-maiden, and because of that Álfr was only partly human. He knew runes and could see some things before they happened, and he could also understand the speech of birds. Álfr was a very wise man, beautiful to look at and with many mistresses, but he was melancholy, and it seemed as if he lived not entirely in the world of men.

Despite what Álfr told Vargrækr, slaying Hjassi was always in the foster brothers' thoughts. Eventually they convinced Vargrækr's father Sjómaðr to raise a great army, and Sjómaðr himself rode out, with all his champions, and Álfr went with them, too, his face painted to resemble a corpse so as to frighten his enemies, and the whole company marched

The blood eagle was a well-known form of execution on the battlefield. First the victim's back would be cut open, and then his ribs would be severed from the spine. Finally, the broken ribs would be pulled through the back along with the lungs, to form a shape resembling a bird's wingspan.

Björgyn is the Old Norse name for the city known today as Bergen.

Dream interpretation was an important feature of the sagas. From Snorre Sturlason's *The Heimskringla: A History of the Norse Kings*:

King Halfdan never had dreams, which appeared to him an extraordinary circumstance; and he told it to a man called Thorleif Spake (the Wise), and asked him what his advice was about it. Thorleif said that what he himself did, when he wanted to have any revelation by dream, was to take his sleep in a swine-sty, and then it never failed that he had dreams. The king did so, and the following dream was revealed to him. He thought he had the most beautiful hair, which was all in ringlets; some so long as to fall upon the ground, some reaching to the middle of his legs, some to his knees, some to his loins or the middle of his sides, and some were only as knots springing from his head… One ringlet surpassed all the others in beauty, luster, and size. This dream he told to Thorleif, who interpreted it thus: There should be a great posterity from him, and his descendants should rule over countries with great, but not all with equally great honor; but one of his race should be more celebrated than all the others. It was the opinion of people that this ringlet betokened King Olaf the Saint.

across Norway to Hjassi where he sat in the court of Vingulmörk. Hjassi saw them coming from afar and gathered all of his army together to meet them, and there they had a tremendous battle, with Sjómaðr's giant army against Hjassi's, which was just as large, and many great and brave deeds were done there, and many lives lost, and many dead bodies littered the ground as food for eagles and ravens. Hjassi's best champions were slain, and many of Sjómaðr's best warriors died also, and in the middle of the tangle of hurled spears and the clatter of swords against armor a Finnish Berserk named Staurask struck Vargrækr's father Sjómaðr so that his sword cleaved through his throat and his chest and into his heart, and Sjómaðr died right there. When they saw this, Eysteinn and Vargrækr fought even more viciously, and when Eysteinn reached Hjassi he swung the sword Svartmálmr over his head and lopped off both of Hjassi's hands at the wrists. But before he could kill Hjassi, Staurask came up and struck Eysteinn, and in this time Hjassi snuck away. Álfr then came to Eysteinn's side and plunged his spear through Staurask's belly even as another of Hjassi's men slashed Álfr across the back with his sword, and Álfr fell down amongst the dead but did not die, and was carried away. This man who had come against Álfr was himself struck down, and the fighting lessened, and Eysteinn again took hold of Vingulmörk.

Hjassi fled north in secret, to Sogn. After losing the battle and all of his warriors, along with both of his hands, he changed in some ways. He no longer went conquering other kingdoms but remained in Sogn and became a follower of Olaf the White, and he accepted the Christian faith which was new then in Norway. To honor the new Christian god, Hjassi built the finest church in Sogn at that time, constructed out of great staves of oak. And he fashioned metal fingers for himself to replace the hands that had been mangled by Svartmálmr.

Berserkers (or *Úlfhéðnar*), sometimes called Odin's Soldiers, were especially fierce and relentless on the battlefield, foregoing armor in favor of wolf pelts. From the *Prose Edda*:

Men rushed forward without armor, were as mad as dogs or wolves, bit their shields, and were strong as bears or wild bulls, and killed people at a blow, but neither fire nor iron told upon themselves. These were called Berserker.

Norway's stave churches, named for the vertical layout of the logs—staves—used to build them, were constructed by missionaries between the tenth and twelfth centuries. The most famous church of the type, Fantoft stavkirke, was burned down in 1992. It is believed that the fire was set by Varg Vikernes, of the black-metal band Burzum.

VI

WINDS OF FUNERAL

As for Vargrækr, the death of his father caused him deep grief. When the battle had finished he didn't say much, only that he felt rage that Hjassi had escaped from Eysteinn's sword and was still alive, and that if Vargrækr had been fighting Hjassi he surely wouldn't have let him escape. Vargrækr's mother Bora was grieved as well, and she never smiled or was happy thenceforth.

Twelve champions bore Sjómaðr's body back to Björgyn, where they laid Sjómaðr in a mound with all his weapons, on a high hill overlooking the western shore of Horðaland, and bent ash branches over him. You can still see traces of this grave, which ever since people have called Sjómaðr's Mound.

After Sjómaðr's burial, the company stayed on in Björgyn for some months, and Vargrækr was silent and mournful. Then, after some time, Vargrækr finally spoke and said to Eysteinn, "With our fathers slain and us the only remnants of our line, we are more like true brothers than ever before. Let's ride out to Vingulmörk, our home." The two friends went with their men back to Eysteinn's court and lived there together and reigned together. Eysteinn married a woman called Vigdís and had a son named Verrfeðrungr. Vargrækr married a woman named Sif and they had two daughters, Signý and Skjaldmær. The two men loved their children and told them stories of the legendary men that had come before them, their fathers Forfaðir Hammerheart and Sjómaðr, and Eysteinn's grandfather Blóðstjarna Venomous, and his great-grandfather Gullinguð Four-Sticks.

Various postmortem customs were practiced throughout pagan Scandinavia. Typically, a warrior would be buried with his weaponry, armor, and sometimes his pets. On rarer occasions, a companion or family would be sacrificed to accompany the fallen to Asgard, the world of the Norse gods.

VII

LET'S FUCKING DIE

It happened one morning that Álfr had a dream that he was leading an army against a great force of frost giants. Every time his sword clashed against a giant's shield it made a melodious tone as of music, and every time he slew one of the giants another one would rise up in its place. And in the middle of the battle, a beautiful woman approaches Álfr on the field and says to him, "You don't belong here, warrior. Your blood is not the blood of these men. You should be fighting on the other side of this battle." Álfr asks the woman how to join the other side of the battle and she tells him, "To release the soul one must die. To find peace inside you must be eternal." When Álfr awoke he went downstairs into the warriors' hall at Vingulmörk, where an ash tree grew out through the ground and into the rafters, and he hanged himself upon this tree, and died.

That day Eysteinn and Vargrækr had been out hunting together in the forests to the east of the fjord. When they came home and found Álfr hanging dead from the tree, Vargrækr was very distraught. He said to Eysteinn, "This is a sorrowful blow, to lose such a noble warrior and friend." Eysteinn told Vargrækr that he would cut down Álfr's body and see to the burial.

When Vargrækr left, Eysteinn reached for the sword Svartmálmr to cut the rope around Álfr's neck, but as soon as his hands touched the steel

Elves (*álfr*, in Old Norse) appear frequently in Norse mythology; in the sagas, half-elf children often become particularly heroic warriors.

The destination in the sagas for those who die without honor is Hel. The *Prose Edda* introduces Hel as the resting place for "evil men," while later suggesting its inhabitants are men "dead of sickness or of old age." Whatever the case, any warrior's ambition would be to reach Asgard.

of the sword it was as if a voice spoke and told him what to do. Eysteinn cut down Álfr and took his body outside and built a small fire. Then he took Svartmálmr and hacked open the top of Álfr's head and cut his brains out of his skull and roasted them on the fire and ate a part of them.

As soon as Eysteinn had eaten some of Álfr's brains, he could understand the speech of birds as Álfr had. There was an eagle that had alighted on a branch by him, eyeing Álfr's corpse. The eagle sang to Eysteinn, saying, "There lies the fallen famous half-elf, half his head gone, now no more than a tale. His powers are yours. Take the broken shards of his skull and make a necklace from them. While wearing this necklace, none will be able to harm you and all armies will fall before you. You will be more famous than all other men, and your name will never be forgotten in the Norse tongue. But your fate will also be Álfr's, and the hour of your death will be nearer than it is for those you love. You will be called Nás-Eysteinn."

Eysteinn decided that he wanted to be powerful and famous more than he wanted a long life, so he did as the eagle told him and took pieces of Álfr's skull and threaded them on long hairs from Álfr's head and made a necklace from them. And Nás-Eysteinn buried Álfr in a certain valley on the far eastern side of the castle, next to a stream near a petrified forest.

VIII

WE'RE GONNA BURN
THIS PLACE TO THE GROUND

It happened just like the eagle told Nás-Eysteinn. He became the most famous man in the region, harrying and conquering all around him and putting much of that part of Norway under his rule. And his friend and foster brother Vargrækr was beside him.

One afternoon, Nás-Eysteinn was eating with his men when the same eagle that had told him to make the skull necklace flew to the window. None of his men could understand the eagle's ancient language, but Nás-Eysteinn heard these words:

> I flew far across this country, finding a church in Sogn.
> Perching on a steeple-point, pecking for food I saw him.
> Here handless he hides, Hjassi your foe.
> Crowing and crying of the Christian god men worship.

When he heard the eagle's song, Nás-Eysteinn went to Vargrækr and said, "It is an embarrassment to my fame and to the honor of us

Magic powers are rarely acquired without a catch: In *The Tale of Toki Tokason*, Toki Tokason (son of Toki, and grandson of Toki the Elder) is granted twice the normal life span, but is cursed never to spend more than a year in one place.

Theories persist that much of the verse dialogue in the original sagas was actually taken from traditional songs or other oral traditions. In this one, many of the verses are based on black-metal lyrics, Øystein Aarseth's in particular.

both that this cowardly Christian, Hjassi Handless, is still alive, and I have discovered where he is hiding. Let us ride there together and finally finish the task of avenging our fathers."

Nás-Eysteinn and Vargrækr called together their champions and gathered their army and drew men from all around the region, and they marched to Sogn. Hjassi held an army there too, and they fought back fiercely. Vargrækr himself was cut many times and grievously scarred and wounded, but throughout the battle no one could hurt Nás-Eysteinn. Arrows missed him and swords glanced off him, and he hacked to bits many of Hjassi's soldiers. Finally the two foster brothers pursued Hjassi into his hall at Sogn, and Vargrækr burned Hjassi alive there with all his followers and his whole court. Nás-Eysteinn and Vargrækr then burned down the church Hjassi had built and burned all the churches in the region down into ashes, which was forty-six churches in all. And they tore down and crumbled all the crosses there, until there was no trace left of Hjassi Handless or his followers or his god.

After the battle, Vargrækr said to Nás-Eysteinn, "Foster brother, you led this battle and you are clearly the greater man between us two. Will you give me Hjassi's lands as my own as compensation for the death of my father Sjómaðr?" But Nás-Eysteinn told him that because he led the battle and because Hjassi had also slain his own family members, he was going to keep Sogn for himself.

IX

COMMUNICATION BREAKDOWN

Now the saga says that, after some time had gone by, Vargrækr's mother Bora went to him and said, "Why is it that all around Norway people talk of your foster brother Nás-Eysteinn and they don't talk of you, when you have done as many great deeds as Nás-Eysteinn and when you yourself killed Hjassi Handless, lighting your torch to his hall and burning down all of his churches? It seems to me that whenever you do some great deed people only talk of Nás-Eysteinn having done it. And why is it that Nás-Eysteinn reigns over all of Vingulmörk and Sogn and you have only the town of Björgyn, which is less than half the size of his land? You were raised as brothers and loved equally by Forfaðir as by Sjómaðr and myself, and you should rule as brothers and share the same power and land equally. Go to Nás-Eysteinn again, and ask him for land of your own to rule over."

So Vargrækr went again to Nás-Eysteinn and asked him, "Foster brother, that you have more wealth and fame than I is disputed by no

Christianity spread slowly in Scandinavia. In *The Saga of Haakon the Good*, King Haakon the Good, an early convert, declares his wish that "the whole public in general, young and old, rich and poor… should believe in one God, and in Christ the son of Mary, and refrain from all sacrifices and heathen gods." His subjects promptly refuse. At the next harvest feast, as diners bless the first goblet in Odin's name, Haakon makes the sign of the cross instead. The table erupts immediately in disbelief and outrage, and is only settled when the king's spokesman of sorts, Earl Sigurd, claims, "The king is doing what all of you do… he is blessing the full goblet in the name of Thor, by making the sign of his hammer over it before he drinks it." King Haakon the Good does not dispute Sigurd's characterization of his motion.

one. I humbly ask for just a small portion of the vast lands over which you rule since defeating Hjassi."

Nás-Eysteinn replied, "You are my dearest friend, but I simply cannot give you this."

When he heard Nás-Eysteinn's words, Vargrækr became angry at him for the first time, wondering why he would humiliate him by denying this one small request. He decided to leave Vingulmörk at once, gathering his wife Sif and their daughters Signý and Skjaldmær. When he saw Vargrækr leaving, Nás-Eysteinn thought twice about having refused him land and offered him anything to stay, but Vargrækr told him it was too late.

X

AN OATH SWORN IN BJÖRGYN

Vargrækr returned to Björgyn and stayed there for some years. He heard daily of Nás-Eysteinn's exploits and of all the land that had fallen under his rule and all the verses and songs that had been composed about him, and daily he grew angrier at his foster brother for not allowing him to share in his land and wealth.

One day Snorri Thorns, the champion of Nás-Eysteinn's court, came to Björgyn to visit Vargrækr, and Vargrækr held a feast to welcome him. After they had been drinking and talking for some time, Snorri asked Vargrækr if he'd heard tales of a necklace Nás-Eysteinn wore in secrecy, which gave him magical abilities and ensured no sword could bite him. Vargrækr told Snorri he hadn't heard of such a necklace, and Snorri replied that no one had known of it until one night Nás-Eysteinn had been boasting of it while drunk. "And here is the reason I am telling you," Snorri said. "I have always believed you to be a greater man than Nás-Eysteinn. I think that the power this necklace confers should be held by you, the warrior who slew Hjassi, and not by one who would lie and conceal his advantage. Nás-Eysteinn has become legendary while wearing this necklace, but if you were to wear it they would make legends about you."

Now the saga says the two made an oath to take Nás-Eysteinn's necklace from him, and Vargrækr traveled with Snorri Thorns from Björgyn to Vingulmörk, and when they arrived there Nás-Eysteinn welcomed them warmly, thinking Vargrækr had forgiven him. The two old friends and foster brothers drank together late into the night, remembering tales of their fathers and grandfathers and their battles and conquests together, until Nás-Eysteinn, having drunk more than Vargrækr, retired to his chamber to sleep. Vargrækr remained awake for

Jealousy is a constant hazard in the genre. *The Saga of the Volsungs* describes how

> Sigi fared to the hunting of the deer, and the thrall Bredi with him; and they hunted deer daylong till the evening; and when they gathered together their prey in the evening, lo, greater and more by far was that which Bredi had slain than Sigi's prey; and this thing he much misliked, and he said that great wonder it was that a very thrall should outdo him in the hunting of deer: so he fell on him and slew him, and buried the body of him thereafter in a snow-drift.

> Then he went home at evening tide and says that Bredi had ridden away from him into the wild-wood. "Soon was he out of my sight," he says, "and naught more I wot of him."

a little while and then, so that no one would recognize him going into Nás-Eysteinn's chamber, he put on a blue cloak with a heavy hood. He tells Snorri, "Wait outside in the hall for me."

Vargrækr enters Nás-Eysteinn's chamber to see him asleep wearing the necklace made from Álfr's skull. He slips the necklace from Nás-Eysteinn's neck and takes a small sword from his belt and stabs Nás-Eysteinn many times, and Nás-Eysteinn awakes and throws the wolf-skin he was sleeping under onto Vargrækr and tries to fight him but he has no weapon, and Vargrækr stabs him twenty-three times in all, and when he was finished he sang this verse:

> Good morning, my foster brother. Meet the face of death.
>
> Sword in hand I'm smiling, seeing your guts stream out.
>
> I first brought war to Hjassi; I burned him alive. Brazenly you
>> stole my deeds.
>
> Now I steal your necklace and your life. No one will ever miss you.

"Well, we all must die one day, and you will too. Valhöll, I am coming," answered Nás-Eysteinn. And, bleeding to death, he made this song:

> I shut my ears to women's sighs, seeking instead blood, fire, and death.
>
> I looked away from light and joy—legends and fame were what I sought.
>
> No light of new morning will come. Even now I'm too old.
>
> I smell that stench already, my soul going as my body rots.
>
> I do remember it, as if from a dream. Darkness grows and eternity opens.
>
> We lifted glasses and laughed, Álfr and Aska and Þræll.
>
> Helhamarr and Helalmáttigr. Bárðr and Ódáinn.
>
> Battle-thirsty Thor Innards-Field, Snorri Thorns (just outside the door).
>
> And, slain by Staurask, Sjómaðr your father who raised us.
>
> My father Forfaðir fallen too. Far-off Eirð also gone.
>
> Blóðstjarna and his brother Blóðlauss—both together now,
>> all wrongs forgotten.
>
> Father of my father's father, Gullinguð. And my foster brother,
>> you, Vargrækr.
>
> In the circle of stone coffins, we are standing with our black robes on.
>
> Everything is cold in the corner of this time, clotted-up and stopped.
>
> But how beautiful life is now, buried by time and dust.
>
> My flesh is a feast for hawks, and flocks of ravens can sip my blood.

When he finished these verses, Nás-Eysteinn died.

After a climactic battle, a dying man will often engage in one last song. In *The Saga of Hervor and King Heidrek the Wise*, Hjalmar's final words are

> I've sixteen wounds,
> a slit byrnie,
> there's clouds before my eyes—
> can't see.
> It entered my heart,
> Angantyr's sword,
> fell bloodspike,
> forged in poison.
>
> I had five
> farms in all,
> but that was never
> enough for me.
> Now I must lie,
> of life deprived,
> sword-maimed,
> on Samsey Isle.

Scandinavian graveyards were arranged in a circle, sometimes with crude uncarved stones to mark the graves at the site of a battle.

XI

RAINING BLOOD

As Snorri Thorns stood guard outside Nás-Eysteinn's chamber, he heard a terrible peal of thunder and the sky broke open into a deafening storm. He ran to the window and looked out to see that what appeared to be rain clouds was a procession of warriors charging across the sky, and so many were their number that the air was almost black, and the rain that fell was blood-red. In the middle of the procession he sees an old man with a wide-brimmed hat, galloping on a black horse with eight legs, and there are bare-breasted women riding at the front of the procession, and birds of prey swooping beneath it. And near the front of this procession Snorri sees the dead warrior Forfaðir, wearing a helm of gold and silver and beating a drum made of human skin. Snorri was so frightened by this vision that he ran downstairs and into the halls of Nás-Eysteinn's sleeping champions and woke them all, telling them that Nás-Eysteinn had been murdered by Vargrækr and pretending to have just discovered the crime.

When Vargrækr heard Nás-Eysteinn's champions running up the stairs after him, he leapt in fear from the window of Nás-Eysteinn's chamber, dropping the skull necklace as he fell so that it shattered on the ground below. Word was sent out that he was to be hunted as a killer-wolf, and he spent the rest of his life in the forests, far from men, and no more is told of him.

All of the Northlands mourned the death of Nás-Eysteinn, and for his funeral he was attired in armor the same gold color as the sun, and laid with the sword Svartmálmr in his hands and a gold shield by his side and placed in a ship, and his champions pushed the ship out to sea, with Ódáinn leading them, also dressed in gold armor, and they set the ship on fire. And Nás-Eysteinn's body burned until all the flesh on it burned up and rose into the gray skies and all that was left were bones, and those bones slipped through the burning planks of his ship as it crumbled and fell apart, and they drifted to the bottom of the same sea that held the bones of his great-uncle, Blóðlauss.

With Nás-Eysteinn murdered by Vargrækr, rulership of Vingulmörk fell to his son, Verrfeðrungr. Verrfeðrungr ruled for a very long time, much longer than the rule of Nás-Eysteinn, or Forfaðir, or Gullinguð, or any of their line, and he did many things, but there is no need to record them. When he died, after a great many years, not in battle but from old age, everyone said that he had ruled the land ably, though it was agreed that he was not as great of a man as his father.

When Valkyries come to earth to fetch slain heroes, they arrive fully armed with swords, spears, and shields, often riding bareback on winged horses or wolves. Sometimes the Valkyries are naked. They are, or at least appear to be, very beautiful.

Verrfeðrungr is Old Norse for "lesser man than his father."

BIJI

LIFE SPAN: 220–1912 AD

NATURAL HABITAT: China

PRACTITIONERS: Duan Chengshi, Ji Yun, Hong Mai,
Zhao Yi, Qian Douxin

CHARACTERISTICS: Musings, anecdotes, quotations,
"believe-it-or-not" fiction, social anthropology

Biji can be translated as "notebook," and a biji can contain legends, short anecdotes, scientific and anthropological notes, and bits of local wisdom. (True to its polyglot form, the biji is known by many names: *xiaoshuo*, *zazu*, *suoyu*, *leishu*, *zalu*.) Accounts of everyday life mix with travel narratives and stories of the supernatural; tales of romance and court intrigue are interspersed with lists of interesting objects or unusual types of food. The unstable styles and irregular content ultimately cohere: between fiction and nonfiction, biji offer a top-down vision of a culture and its time.

YOUYANG ZAZU

a biji by DUAN CHENGSHI

—C. 830 AD—

Duan Chengshi, the son of a wealthy politician, spent much of his life traveling through Tang-dynasty China. One of several biji he composed, the Youyang zazu *("Miscellaneous Morsels from the South Slope of You Mountain") forms a panoramic portrait of the world he saw, collecting observations, local legends, brief glimpses of everyday life, and intimations of the beyond.*

N THE DAY of the Establishing Spring, the emperor bestows upon the attendant officers trees with multicolored flowers.

o

Taizong had curly whiskers. He sometimes used to amuse himself by stretching a bow and fitting arrows to his string. He preferred to use a four-feathered broad arrow shaft, longer than most arrows by a length. He could shoot an arrow through a hole in a door leaf.

o

Among the one hundred horses that the nation of Kourikan presented to the throne, ten were exceptional steeds, and the emperor named them. [Though] there were shackles near the hind hoofs of the horse called

Roan Wave-breaker, the horse could run over the gate's three thresholds without stumbling. The emperor especially cherished this horse. In the inner treasury of the Sui dynasty there used to be a carved jade ape with crossed arms. The two arms were threaded together like connecting rings; this ornament was meant to be displayed on the reins of a horse. Once at a later time the emperor was riding with his attendant officers. He hated that rein ornament so he beat it to pieces with his whip.

木飲州珠崖一州其地無泉民不作井皆仰樹汁為用

木僕尾若龜長數寸居木上食人

阿薩部多獵蚊鹿剖其肉重疊之以石壓瀝汁

稅波斯拂菻等國米及草子釀於肉汁之中經數日即

麼成酒飲之可醉

孝億國界周三千餘里在平川中以木為柵周十餘里

柵內百姓二十餘家周國大柵五百餘所氣候常暖

冬不凋落宜年馬無駞牛俗性質直好客侶軀貌長

欽定四庫全書　酉陽雜俎　卷四　三

大宴鼻黃髪綠眼赤髭被面如血色戰具唯稍一

色宜五穀出金鐵衣麻布舉俗事妖不識佛法有妖

祠三百十一口餘所馬步甲兵一萬不尚商販自稱孝

億人丈夫婦人俱帶每一日造食一月食之常喫宿

仍建國無井及河澗所有種植待雨而生以紫鑛泥地

承雨水用之穿井即若海水又鹹土俗潮落之後平

地為池取魚以作食

食

Toward the end of the Tianbao era Indochina offered as a tribute a present of the Dragon Brain Aromatic. It was carved into the shapes of cicadas and silkworms. In the inner apartments of the palace they call it "Auspicious Dragon Brain." The emperor exclusively bestowed ten pieces of it upon Yang Guifei, and the fragrance penetrated to a distance of more than ten paces. Once, on a summer's day, the emperor was playing chess with a prince of the royal family, and he ordered He Huaizhi to play a solo on the pipa. Guifei stood in front of their game board watching them play. When several of the emperor's pieces were about to be lost, Guifei let loose a Samarkandian toy dog from its place next to her. The dog upset the game board, the pieces were sent into disarray and the emperor was greatly pleased. At that moment the wind blew Guifei's neck scarf on to the kerchief of He Huaizhi. After quite a long time, it fell off when he turned his body around. When He Huaizhi went home, he became aware that his whole body was suffused with an extraordinary fragrance. He then took off his headgear and put it away in a brocade bag. When it came time for the emperor to return to the palace gates, he never ceased thinking about Guifei. He Huaizhi then brought out the kerchief which he had stored away. He fully laid out the details of that earlier day. His Imperial Majesty opened the bag and wept, saying, "This is the Auspicious Dragon Brain Aromatic!"

o

There are seventy-five grades of ghostly offices. There are nine ranks of immortals. The Great Emperors number twenty-seven, the Heavenly Lords number twelve hundred, the Palaces of Immortals number twenty-four hundred. There are thirty-two Offices of Transcendants, and three grades, nine grades, and seven cities of the Arbiters of Destiny. There are nine levels, twenty-seven ranks, and seventy-two thousand gradations.

o

Eastern people have big noses. Their intelligence is linked to the eyes. Muscular strength is associated with them. Southern people have big mouths, and their intelligence is linked to their ears. Westerners have big faces, and their intelligence is linked to their noses. The intelligence of Northerners is linked to their genitals and their short necks. The intelligence of people of central regions is linked to their mouths.

Translated by Carrie E. Reed. Image from the Youyang zazu.

SURVIVOR

a new biji by DOUGLAS COUPLAND

FUCKING *FUCK*, THERE IS no place worse than the port side of the Luxurious CBS Yacht. Each morning I'm greeted by sauna-like humidity and the perpetual odor of tuna sandwiches, plus, believe it or not, the sound of CBS executives playing racquetball. Their court is on the other side of my headboard's wall. Thank you, British divorce laws, for handing me this sack-of-shit career move. We're in the middle of fucking nowhere and sleep doesn't even provide me with dreams, just an escape from those sniveling American shits I now have to shadow all day. Could these people have found a place on earth more remote? Excuse me, but were the Kerguelen Islands all booked up? Did Pitcairn Island shut down for an extended religious holiday? I tried Google-mapping this place: Fucking fuckity *fuck*.

o

We are sorry, but we don't have maps at this zoom level for this region.

Try zooming out for a broader look.

Divorces can result in bizarre, sometimes insulting settlements in a biji. In the *Nuogao ji* ("Records of Nuogao"), another biji written by Duan Chengshi, a young girl marries a creature that is not exactly human. Two years later, the creature—called a Yaksha—tells her that he is leaving her:

> Then he gave her a blue-green stone, as big as a hen's egg, and he said that when she got home she could grind it up and take it as medicine. She would thus be able to overcome his poisonous influence… Her mother ground up the stone, and gave it to her to drink. In the bottom of the glass there was more than a dipperful of something like green mud.

○

The Republic of Kiribati is an island nation located in the central Pacific Ocean. It comprises thirty-two atolls and one raised coral island, and is spread over 1.4 million square miles. Kiribati straddles the equator and, on its east side, borders the international date line. Its former colonial name was the Gilbert and Ellice Islands. The capital and largest city is South Tarawa.

OFFICIAL LANGUAGES: English, Gilbertese
POPULATION: 105,000
GDP: $206 million
INTERNET TOP-LEVEL DOMAIN (TLD): .ki
INTERNATIONAL CALLING CODE: +686

○

Naming, and renaming, are also discussed in the *Nuogao ji*:

> The Mountain Artemesia in one source is also named the Mountain Rankness. The *Shen yijing* calls it Shan shan. The *Yong jia jun ji* calls it the Mountain Demon, and one source calls it the Mountain Camel, and one calls it the Jiao Dragon. One source calls it Dazzling Meat, one calls it Cooked Meat. One calls it Radiant, and one calls it Flying Dragon… If its nest is invaded it employs tigers to kill people, and it burns people's homes. It is commonly known as the Mountain Sprite.

Our ludicrous contestants had to choose names for their "tribes" today. I suggested Swallowers versus Spitters and got pursed lips all around. Fucking Americans: no sense of humor. Doubtless they all own *Forrest Gump* on DVD and have already asked each other what they want to be when they grow up. They are monsters.

○

Kiribati has few natural resources. Commercially viable phosphate deposits were exhausted at the time of its 1979 independence. Copra (dried coconut kernels) and fish now represent the bulk of production and exports. Tourism provides more than one-fifth of the country's GDP.

○

In 1908, Jack London wrote an article entitled "The Lepers of Molokai" for *Woman's Home Companion* magazine. In it, London wrote, "Leprosy is terrible, there is no getting away from that… but if it were given to me to choose between being compelled to live in Molokai for the rest of my life, or in the East End of London, the East Side of New York, or the Stock Yards of Chicago, I would select Molokai without debate."

I have eight fellow cameramen, five of them veteran crew members of this wretched show. They divide contestants into two categories: Fuckable and Unfuckable. They treat the latter like Molokai lepers. As far as I can see, our biggest technical issue is ensuring that our shadows not appear on the sand—very hard to do around sunrise and sunset.

○

Survivor is a popular reality-TV game show, versions of which have been produced in many different countries. In the show, contestants are isolated in the wilderness and compete for cash and other prizes. The show uses a progressive elimination, allowing the contestants to vote off tribe members until only one remains and wins the title of "Sole Survivor."

The initial U.S. series was a huge ratings success in 2000 and triggered a reality-TV revolution in the USA.

○

Last night I got saddled with infrared night-shift filming. Ray, a fellow Brit cameraman, told me it's too early in the season for the contestants to truly fuck around, and I was prepared for eight hours of drying paint when a storm came out of nowhere and blasted away the pathetic huts they'd made as shelters. Talk about sniveling! *So* much fun to see them get what they deserve. The Spitters also inadvertently spilled their rice canister. When they picked it up, it had become a big white lump filled with dead sand flies. It looked like raisin-bread dough. They are going to starve and it's going to be very funny.

Ray tells me that it usually takes about three storms before the contestants discreetly offer blow jobs in return for chocolate bars, bug repellant, and antifungal sprays. Perhaps there *is* light at the end of this tunnel.

Am feeling a bit ill. Too much sun is getting to me, I think.

○

Traveler's Alert

Lymphatic filariasis
Dengue-4 virus
Soil-transmitted helminths
Parastrongylus cantonensis
Plasmodium berghei
Trypanosoma cruzi
Leishmaniasis
Schistosomiasis
Multidrug-resistant *falciparum*
Simulium (Gomphostilbia) palauense

○

Tomorrow is my day off—a whole day on the Luxurious CBS Yacht, alone and getting shitfaced! Please, dear God, let me slit my wrists now.

There is a chance I may get to chopper in to the main town on the big island—which actually sounds interesting in a let's-go-whoring kind of way. Ray tells me the Kiribatese women all weigh five hundred pounds and have multiple diabetic amputations, but I find that hard to believe.

Biji often contained health-related advice, mainly simple remedies for common ailments and folkloric methods of warding off danger. In the *Youyang zazu*, Duan Chengshi writes:

> On the third day of the third month the emperor bestows upon the attendant officials slender willow wreaths. It is said that if you wear one of these at your waist, it will protect you from the poison of scorpions.

The people of Kiribati are actually called I-Kiribati, not Kiribatese.

○

The *Youyang zazu* mentions another sort of capital city: "The Wasteland of Kunlun is the lesser capital of the gods. It is the dwelling place of hundreds of spirits."

South Tarawa is the official capital of the Republic of Kiribati. The South Tarawa population center consists of the small islets between Bairiki (on the west) and Bonriki (on the east). The once-separate islets are joined by causeways, forming one long islet along the southern side of the Tarawa Lagoon. The Parliament meets on Ambo islet; various ministries are scattered between South Tarawa, Betio, and Christmas Island.

○

My trip to Tarawa? A disaster. The plump, churchy Kiribati girls are apparently immune to my considerable northern-hemispheric charms. I didn't expect a clusterfuck on the high street, but I certainly wasn't expecting dead, frosty stares in return for a flirty goosing here and there. Fucking church. It'll be wanking for me tonight.

The *Nuogao ji* records a strategy for finding a mate with the help of a certain water spirit, which had a habit of drowning beautiful women as they crossed its river:

Those women who did not cause the wind to whip up the waves considered that it was because they were ugly that they did not incur the wrath of the water spirit. Therefore, the people of Qi have a saying which goes, "If you want to find a good wife, stand at the mouth of the ford. When a woman stands next to the water, her beauty or ugliness will manifest itself."

I spent the time I'd allotted for whoring walking around enjoying a litter-festooned pseudoparadise. Its only charms for the casual visitor are the wide array of luncheon meats available in the general store, and nonradioactivity. I'm told this is one of the few atolls around here that didn't get fried by the Americans or the French back in the sixties and seventies.

○

Pacific Proving Grounds was the name used to describe a number of sites in the Marshall Islands which were used by the United States to conduct nuclear tests between 1946 and 1962. Sixty-seven atmospheric tests were conducted there, many of which were of extremely high yield. The largest test was the fifteen-megaton Castle Bravo shot of 1954, which spread considerable nuclear fallout on many of the islands.

○

Tuna Schnitzel
Tuna steak in breadcrumbs,
served with potato chips
and cucumber slices.

Tuna Salad
Raw tuna fish with onions in a spicy sauce.
Served with crusty bread.

Tuna Tartare
Raw tuna fish minced together
with hot spices,
spread onto garlic bread.

○

Vomited up lunch on the side of the grandly named Dai-Nippon Causeway (it's just a road) and was nearly run over by a rusted-out 1982 Chrysler LeBaron driven by some tubby local whose future is doomed by a diet based almost solely on tropical oils and the absence of any form of education.

○

There was a delay with the chopper back to the Luxurious CBS Yacht: apparently the price of gas tripled last night. The marine fuel pumps were guarded by three morbidly obese thugs in purple T-shirts toting rifles. Not something you see every day. Fucking OPEC. I've never felt this far away from civilization in my life. And what awaits me on the Yacht but booze, body lotion, a hand towel, and my right hand—or my left hand, if I want to make it seem like it's someone else.

○

We're down to eleven contestants now. They are:

1. Blonde slut.

2. Other blonde slut.

3. Third blonde slut inside whose chest exist two proud examples of Nena's drifting *neun-und-neunzig luftballons.*

4. Brunette slut.

5. Black guy.

6. Gay guy.

7. Waste-of-space nerd.

8. Scary, well-nourished upper-middle-class woman who would really be better off concealing her wattles beneath a Katharine Hepburn–style beekeeper's hat (and preferably also being on some other show).

9. Worthy black woman who will be eaten alive by a clique of young white people.

10. Dumb hunk.

11. Noble hunk (FDNY).

○

Lists were a common feature of the original scrolls. The *Youyang zazu* catalogs the imperial gifts that one man from eighth-century China received:

1. Sangluo wine.
2. Musk of the Broadtailed sheep.
3. Koumiss cheese.
4. Two troupes of singers.
5. Wild boar preserves.
6. Bream fish along with a hand knife for mincing the fish.
7. Sacrificial wine.
8. Great brocade.
9. Precious *zhenfu* chariot made of butter.
10. *Amalaka* extract.
11. Pheasant from Liaodong.
12. Five-techniques soup.
13. One measure of "pure water," along with *xixianzi* of the *Yaotong*, to send along to the new residence to make a decoction.

Other instances of the disappearance of birds as a symbol of death can be found in biji. In the *Youyang zazu*, Duan Chengshi writes,

> One of Gu Kuang's sons died at the age of seventeen. The soul of this son wandered, irresolute, as if in a dream, and did not leave their home. Gu Kuang was so constantly mournful that he made up a poem and intoned it as he cried. The poem went:

> This old man lost one son,
> With the setting of the sun, my tears flow like blood.
> Whenever I hear the ape's sad cries
> I am startled.
> His tracks vanished like birds in flight.
> I am an old man of seventy; we shall not be apart for long.

> When Gu's son heard the poem, he was moved to sorrow, and he vowed to himself immediately that he would take a human body and be born into the Gu household again...

I just found out from an assistant that when we choppered in yesterday afternoon, we flew too low over a breeding colony of endangered red-tipped auks, and most of them ate their chicks in response. By Jove, nature is majestic.

○

Dumb Hunk and Brunette Slut were about to get it on in a plumeria glade when Ray and I got a transmission to come back to the Luxurious CBS Yacht, with the addendum that all shooting for the day was over. Ray, a veteran of eight seasons, said that something like this had never before happened.

Once onboard, we learned that all transmissions to the outside world had stopped at 9:31 p.m. London time. As well, satellite links to the airport in Kiribati were down. We tried any other number of links, but nothing.

○

Southern Cross Cables to NZ, Hawaii, Fiji, and U.S. mainland
Australia–Japan Cable
Indonesian Sea-Me-We3 and Jasaurus links
Papua New Guinea APNG2 link
PPC-1 and Sanchar Nigam links into Guam
Hawaiian Telestra links
Gondwana link from New Caledonia to Australia
Intelsat
Inmarsat
SingTel Optus Earth stations

○

Went back to my wretched portside bedsit for a vodka hit. I tried going online, but of course the Internet was out. So I lay back on my bed, attempted to mentally erase the smell of tuna sandwiches, and stared at a map of Southeast Asia. For the first time ever, I looked at the Philippines. I looked at the word over and over.

> *Philippines*
> *Philippines*
> *Philippines*
> *Philippines*
> Who the fuck was Philipp?

○

Went back upstairs to the bar at the stern of the Luxurious CBS Yacht and everybody was getting hammered. At sunset the tech guy received a weak signal from somewhere and apparently the American air-force base in Guam was nuked by we-know-not-who. Nukes all over the place, like Chinese New Year. Even meek little Auckland, New Zealand got whacked. Nuking New Zealand is like nuking Narnia—and not at all sporting of whoever launched the bombs.

Debate raged as to whether or not we should tell the contestants about world events; we decided, in the absence of anything else constructive to do, to continue shooting. For the night we agree to leave the contestants unobserved and incommunicado. They're so used to having their every whine recorded that the absence of cameras will be very disorienting indeed. Let them sweat it out, for once.

I returned to bed passed-out drunk.

o

Woke up with acrid vomit rising up my throat and into my sinus cavities. Right, I'd bought six Ambiens from Jerry, the guy with Asperger's down in the editing suite. I'd forgotten the most important maxim of life in the media: booze + pills + full stomach + sleep = rock-star death. Cliché or not, I really thought I was going to accidentally drown in my own vomit there on my cabin floor, but was able to gargle and sneeze and get everything out just in time. This made me happy not only because I continue to be alive, but also because it was Bug-Eating Contest Day, when contestants eat technically nontoxic but nonetheless motherfucker local insects. Whoever eats the most in two minutes wins a saccharine DVD of friends and family members rooting for them back home. Fucking Americans. Family this, family that, *Tell Mom I love her, I love you all so much*—they're like children. Maybe we should show them a satellite clip of Auckland, New Zealand roasting in a landscape of radioactive magma instead.

To get us all in the right mood, Autistic Jerry showed us some YouTube clips he'd saved on his hard drive of people at home using their blenders to make insect smoothies.

o

http://www.youtube.com/watch?v=SWIBp0IrXEE
http://www.youtube.com/watch?v=1AzYmJiVDqU
http://www.youtube.com/watch?v=__srsDMKo9k

The *Nuogao ji* describes another type of deadly long-range weapon—a magical stalk of grass that only a creature called a Fengli knows how to obtain. Any person who wants to wield it waits in hiding for days, until the Fengli is sure it is alone, at which point it will procure the stalk and point it at nesting birds. The birds fall from their perches, and the Fengli eats them. Meanwhile:

> The people wait for it to become off guard, then run with all their strength to capture the stalk. When it sees people, it slowly gnaws on its stalk of grass and eats it. Sometimes, when there is not enough time for that, it will throw it into the grass. If the people can't get hold of the stalk, they will beat the Fengli several hundred times. For this reason the Fengli began to be willing to fetch it for these people. As for those who have captured a Fengli's stalk, whatever bird or beasts they point at will die. Whatever they wish for, they have only to point at it, and they will have it.

o

Hi Lisa!

How are you, Sweetie? We miss you here back home, but we know you're down there being the best Survivor ever. Are you eating enough? Are you outwitting, outsmarting, and outlasting everybody? Have you had the bug-eating contest yet? Bleccch! How can you people do stuff like that? Well, anything to win! Not much to report. Schooner here really misses you, right Schooner? Looks like Schooner's not in a talkative mood today. *Where's Lisa? Where's Lisa? Talk to Lisa!* Just go on winning your game, sweetheart, and know how much we love you and miss you—and if you don't win the million-dollar prize, we'll still love you, right Schooner?

Bye Sweetie
Love you

o

The types of challenges that *Survivor* contestants engage in have an analogous predecessor in the *Youyang zazu*. Describing the tribal activities of the ancestors of the Turks, Duan Chengshi writes:

> Some time later, just as the tribe was preparing for a great hunt, at nightfall the sea spirit's daughter said to She Mo, "Tomorrow at the hunt out from the cave in which your ancestors were born should come a white deer with golden antlers. If you shoot and kill this deer, you will be permitted to continue seeing me for the rest of your life. If your shot does not kill the deer, the visits will immediately come to an end."

Our bug-eating shoot was interrupted when I tripped over a root and got an avocado branch javelined directly into my right calf. Fucking *fuck*. I took the chopper into Tarawa along with three CBS execs intent on flying home, which, given that the northern hemisphere is most likely a glowing charcoal briquette at the moment, didn't seem to be too swift a decision on their part. But as it turned out their choice to flee was moot. When we arrived to the airport, even a cretin could see that nobody was going anywhere; planes were strewn all over the tarmac like children's toys on a playroom floor. It had just rained, and the tarmac didn't look wet so much as it did like a big dog had pissed on it.

We landed over by a huge mesh fence at the airport's western edge. A passing Air Pacific flight attendant, the luscious "Teehee," just in from a long haul from Singapore and a bit frazzled—hair sticking out in all directions—told us to stay near the helicopter, and this did make intuitive sense, as on the other side of the mesh were maybe a hundred tourists with duffel bags and hastily packed luggage pleading to get into the airport and onto any flight they could.

I stayed in the chopper, injecting myself with morphine; my Spidey senses were tingling and I wasn't planning on going anywhere I didn't have to. The CBS execs, on the other hand, made the mistake of going into one of the corrugated zinc Quonset buildings that turned out to be the customs and immigration shed; they weren't allowed back out. Our pilot, Alan, had been smoking a cigarette out on the tarmac when the execs started screaming. He sprinted back to the chopper, and within thirty seconds we were airborne. "There's no way you want to be down in that rat's nest, mate," he said to me. "And if you ask me, there's not going to be many flights to Brisbane for the next hundred years. Be a mate and reach into that bag over there and get my bottle of cognac. I could use a little lift right now."

As I looked down I saw a quartet of Air Nauru flight attendants throwing conch shells at the angry mob on the other side of the fence, the shells shattering as they hit the fence's metal weave, turning to chalk.

o

Is there ever such thing as a mob that *isn't* angry? Or would one simply call that a "crowd"? Is an angry crowd de facto a mob?

o

Flight 311: Nauru–Honiara–Brisbane

Departs Nauru:	06:45	Delayed
Arrives Honiara:	07:30	Delayed
Departs Honiara:	08:15	Delayed
Arrives Brisbane:	10:30	Delayed

o

In my absence, the Luxurious CBS Yacht polarized into two factions: fuckfest upstairs, gloom and tears and sniveling downstairs. Needless to say, as soon as I got back I was upstairs gorging on a feast of muscle relaxants and pity sex. Thank you, avocado branch, for rendering me fuckable in the eyes of comely production assistants.

The only bad news was Dan "The Danimal," our L.A.-based cameraman, who hanged himself from the beams of a ridiculous bamboo contraption designed for tomorrow's archery-based rewards challenge. Sissy. Battle scars or not, tomorrow I'm on day-camera duty.

o

How to Calculate Your Total Daily Calorie Needs

STEP 1: Multiply your current weight in pounds by ten if you're a woman, or by eleven if you're a man. This number represents your basic calorie needs.

STEP 2: Multiply your basic calorie needs by your activity level—20 percent (or 0.2) if you sit or lie still for most of the day, with little

Biji commonly discussed violent deaths in blunt terms. From the *Youyang zazu*:

Palace Attendant Ma once treasured a fine jade bowl. In summer flies would not go near it. If he filled it up with water, a month could pass and the water would not go bad, nor would it diminish in quantity... Once Ma put it in a box in his bedroom, and a small slave of seven or eight years of age secretly played with it and broke it... When Ma discovered that the bowl had been broken, he was greatly enraged... He said, "Breaking my bowl was an insignificant thing." But then he ordered his associates to beat the slave to death.

or no exercise; 30 percent if you walk less than two miles per day; 40 percent if you are somewhat active, doing activities such as dancing, doing a lot of work in the house or garden, or taking exercise classes; and 50 percent if you're actively involved in a sport or you have a job that requires a great deal of physical labor, such as construction work. The resulting number reflects your activity-based calorie needs.

STEP 3: Add your basic calorie needs from steps 1 and 2, then multiply this sum by 0.1—these are the calories you need for digestion.

STEP 4: Combine the results from steps 1, 2, and 3: This is your total daily calorie need to maintain your weight!

o

Well, here we are. The contestants found out about whatever it is, nuclear war or what have you, and our resulting inability to communicate with the rest of the world. To their credit, they figured it out by noticing a change in crew behavior (hangover, lack of poker face) and the fact that there were fewer of us (B-camera crew, set-dec, and props department, plus half the sound staff on a two-day mini-holiday, all incinerated in the Guam Hotel Nikko).

There were the eleven of them and eight or nine of us standing at the edge of a glorious sapphire lagoon when it came out. The contestants looked like they'd been clubbed.

Then there was this eerie minute where nobody spoke, which lasted until the two chickens that had escaped from the previous week's reward challenge began taunting us with their cackles and shrieks from up in the palmetto scrub.

Couldn't wait to return to the Luxurious CBSY.

o

The LCBSY is gone. Ray and I got into our Zodiac near sunset, having talked down a slim majority of the contestants, then circled the island to where the yacht ought to have been only to find that it *was not there*. We could have gone searching for it, but when the sun goes down in the Pacific it's like an off switch.

We ended up overnighting on one of the tinier islands, both of us starving. Upon waking, five bodies had washed ashore in the night: Asperger's Jerry, two production assistants, the chef, and the lone CBS executive who'd stayed behind. Things are not going to get better here.

Duan Chengshi, in the *Youyang zazu*, on what not to eat, and on what to eat to save your life if you eat what not to eat:

Northern creeper grass grows in Yong and Rong. It grows in thickets. The flowers are flat like those of the gardenia but are a bit bigger. They do not form in a cluster. The color is yellowish white. The leaves are partly black. If you mistakenly eat the grass, you will die within several days, but if you drink the blood of a white goose or a white duck, the poison will dissipate. Sometimes people throw something at this plant and say in incantation, "I buy you." Then, if someone eats it, he will immediately die.

○

There's a part of me that loves the prospect of lawlessness, I have to admit.

○

Kiribati is a constitutional multiparty republic, and the Kiribati government works to respect the civil and human rights of its citizens. There are only a few areas in which problems remain, but in general, Kiribati's laws provide effective means of addressing individual complaints, although there have been some reports of extrajudicial communal justice.

○

We were going to bury our fellow TV comrades but then decided, why the fuck bother? The sand crabs and the gulls will give the corpses a swift and environmentally friendly end.

Food for Ray and me is a different thing. We spent a few hours trying to decide whether we should go to the Swallowers' campsite, where we left the gang of twenty—or if we should avoid them altogether. As far as we can estimate, there's zero food on any of our surrounding islands (islets, really) unless one of the sound technicians has a granola bar tucked into his knapsack. The nearest inhabited island is a good hour away by boat, and going there would eat up all the gas in our Zodiac. And with gas currently being the most precious local commodity, it's doubtful any of the Kiribatese will be coming to visit or pillage our sad little society here. We are, pardon my French, *totalement fuckés*.

In the end Ray and I decided it would be fun to do a quick cruise past the inhabited island just to remind them that we have a Zodiac and gasoline, whereas they have nothing—certainly no survival skills. I think one or two of them knows how to light a fire, but that's it.

So anyway, after our deeply satisfying strafing of Loser's Island, Ray and I discussed that old TV show *Gilligan's Island*, where six essentially clueless people plus one intelligent professor assembled a reasonable facsimile of civilization from palm fronds and whatever drifted into their lagoon. Surely all of them should have succumbed to rape, buggery, murder, cannibalism, and suicide long before they cobbled together a small Club Med–ish village.

Fucking TV.

○

It's now three foodless days later, and the skin surrounding the interim

Duan Chengshi's advice in the *Youyang zazu* extends mostly to what food to avoid, rather than where to find it:

> If you eat a melon that has two tips and two stems, it will kill you. Violets with yellow flowers, along with red mustard, will kill people. As for gourds, if a cow treads on their sprouts, the fruit will suffer. When one is very drunk, one must not sleep on millet stalks.

Even a properly cared-for wounded limb can take a turn for the worse in a biji. The *Nuogao ji* relates this story:

> Youxuan showed him his elbow, and the old man said, "I happen to have a fine medicine with which I can heal this. You mustn't take the bandage off for ten days; then it will definitely get better." Youxuan did as he was told. When he untied the bandage to get a better look at it, his whole arm fell off.

stitches on my calf are starting to turn all purple and yellow. There's some bloatiness happening. Worst of all, I can't muster the energy or sense of purpose to wank. Before nuclear war my thinking used to be along the lines of, "Sure, right now I'm wanking, but this is just a pale substitute for some genuine bonking I hope to do in the near future." But with no possible bonking available in the near—or distant—term, the sterility and pointlessness of wanking is all too apparent.

And did I mention boredom on top of the starvation and wankless-ness? Half-jokingly Ray suggested we Zodiac to the international date line and go back and forth across it and hence go back and forth in time.

o

On January 1, 1995, the Republic of Kiribati introduced a change of date for its eastern half, from time zones −11 and −10 to +13 and +14. Before this, the country was divided by the date line. A consequence of this revision was that Kiribati, by virtue of its easternmost possession, the uninhabited Caroline Atoll at 150°25 west, started the year 2000 before any other country on Earth, a feature the Kiribati government capitalized upon as a potential tourist draw. The international time-keeping community, however, has not taken this date-line adjustment seriously, noting that most world atlases ignore the new Kiribati date-line shift.

o

One more body washed up (or the remains of one)—Lee-Anne, the makeup woman whom we were able to identify only because the sea creatures who'd nibbled away most of her didn't like the taste of her hippie chunky wood necklace.

o

Ji Yun, in his *Guwang tingzhi* ("Listen in a Rough Way"), notes that the body after death can change in ways beyond decomposition:

> Human beings cannot create something out of nothing, make small things big, or transform what is hideous into a thing of beauty. [But] according to the various books that record encounters with ghosts, coffins are turned into palaces, in which humans can dwell. The ghosts of those who die an unnatural death can assume beautiful appearances. Could it be that once they become ghosts, they acquire such powers? Or are they taught to do so?

QUESTION: What is "grave wax"?

ANSWER: Grave wax is a crumbly, white, waxy substance that accumulates on those parts of the body that contain fat—the cheeks, breasts, abdomen, and buttocks. It is the product of a chemical reaction in which fats react with water and hydrogen in the presence of bacterial enzymes, breaking down into fatty acids and soaps. Grave wax is resistant to bacteria and can protect a corpse, slowing further decomposition. Grave wax starts to form within a month after death and has been recorded on bodies that have been exhumed after one hundred years. If a body is readily accessible to insects, grave wax is unlikely to form.

○

During last night's storm (which we spent beneath the upturned Zodiac, thank you) Ray and I were jokingly discussing who among the twenty on Loser's Island would be the most delicious to eat, and then suddenly the discussion turned serious, which was frightening. My kidneys have shriveled into little raisins by now, and my calf is beginning to resemble beef jerky. Our one conclusion is that we wouldn't touch Other Blonde with Implants—something just too unappetizing about those two silicone blancmanges.

So tomorrow we go.

○

We woke up to a spooky sight: a U.S. battleship drifting past the island, the USS *Ronald Reagan*. At first we thought we were rescued, but after some waving and halloo-ing we dug out our binoculars and saw that there was nobody on deck. And then it got caught in a swell and, over the course of a half hour, turned 180 degrees, and we saw that its starboard side had been scorched or melted or something-or-othered by a nuclear blast. Anybody onboard would have been irradiated to pieces on the spot.

And then… and then it drifted away, off toward Antarctica.

○

Cannibalism is mentioned in the *Nuogao ji* as well:

> After the third watch an old man appeared out of nowhere, dressed all in white, with two fangs protruding beyond his lips. He stared for a long while at the boy; then he gradually approached the front of the bed. A servant girl lay sleeping soundly at the head of the bed, and the old man grasped her by the throat. There was a crunching sound as he ripped her clothes in shreds with his hands. He seized her and gobbled her up, and in no time at all the girl's bare bones were sticking out. Then he lifted what remained of her and swallowed her five organs. Seeing that the old man's mouth was the size of a winnowing basket, the boy shouted out, but as soon as he had done so, the man was nowhere to be seen. The servant was already only a pile of bones.

USS *Ronald Reagan*

AIRCRAFT CARRIED:	Ninety fixed-wing and helicopters
MOTTO:	"Peace Through Strength"
NICKNAME:	"Gipper"
DISPLACEMENT:	101,000 to 104,000 tons full load
LENGTH—OVERALL:	1,092 ft (333 m)
LENGTH—WATERLINE:	1,040 ft (317 m)
PROPULSION:	2 × Westinghouse A4W nuclear reactors
	4 × steam turbines
	4 × shafts 260,000 shp (194 MW)
SPEED:	30+ knots (56+ km/h)
RANGE:	Essentially unlimited
COMPLEMENT:	Ship's company: 3,200
AIR WING:	2,480

○

The next reward challenge was to have been something involving archery; if nothing else, the citizens of Loser's Island are armed. And yes, I'd prefer not to be shot *or* have the Zodiac's neoprene skin be compromised. So yes, we were wary as we neared.

Through binoculars we could see from a quarter mile away that there was nobody visible near the main camp. We circled the island 90 degrees, cut the engine, and scrutinized not just the beaches but the shrubbery and the trees. Nobody. Ray said they all must have passed the point where they were awaiting rescue and moved inland, which made me call him a simpleton, my point being that there's nothing in the middle of these islands but nasty scrub, tarantulas, and spiky plants. Our ultimate conclusion was that even if the Losers were lying in wait with their bows and arrows, they'd keep us alive to see if we had any news.

So this was our chance to give false news to our advantage.

○

The *Youyang zazu* on the use of insects to determine time of death:

> People say that when a person is about to die, lice leave his body. Some people say that if you place the sick person's lice in front of the sick bed, you can tell the course that the illness will take. If he is about to recover, the lice will move toward the afflicted. If they turn away from him, it means that he is going to die.

The presence of insects in a corpse is critical in estimating the time of death of bodies dead over longer time periods. Flies quickly find bodies, and as their life cycles are predictable, a corpse's time of death can be calculated by counting back the days from the state of development of insects within said corpse. Weather conditions can sometimes vary results, and identification of specific maggot species can be difficult.

Here is an example: If a body is found in an air-conditioned building (68°F) with second-instar larvae of *Lucilia sericata* feeding on the corpse, we can calculate that those larvae had molted from their first instar in the previous twelve hours. Because the eggs take eighteen hours to hatch and the first instar takes twenty hours to develop, the most recent time the eggs could have been laid would be thirty-eight hours earlier, if the larvae had just molted. If they were old larvae, about to molt into their third instar, the most recent time of death would be fifty hours prior to the discovery of the body.

○

Remember Jonestown? I certainly do, and I imagine the initial investigators on the scene must have felt something akin to what we did upon beaching on Loser's Cove. From five hundred feet away? Paradise. But once you're on land and walking toward the encampment? Carnage. To be specific, carnage mixed with camera and sound equipment. And unlike Jonestown, where bodies were kind enough to allay themselves in neat rows, here everybody seems to have simply died wherever, like puppets when the hand is removed. And also, unlike Jonestown, the sixteen bodies at the camp seem to have been murdered. Some by strangulation, some by machete—although it's hard to tell if they were killed here, or if the bodies were dragged over. The rains have washed away that sort of evidence.

By using sticks in the sand, we tried to determine if there were any others still out there. In our minds it had always been twenty of them here, cast and crew, but on close inspection the number was actually seventeen. Which meant there was still one survivor. By laborious deduction we determined it to be Michelle, the Brunette Slut, who at that moment might well have been within an arrow's reach of us.

I said, "Ray, maybe it's best we nab some of this camera equipment and take it to a different island. I'd bet the footage has stories to tell us."

"Righty-O," he said.

The presence of footage offered, if nothing else, the prospect of relief from the crushing boredom of island living, although I did wish the camp had had some food to pillage. We were starving.

To look on the bright side of things, God bless the Zodiac crew for leaving both morphine and powerful sedatives in the first-aid kit. Without them I'd be fucked over a hundred times.

o

Risperdal (Risperidone)

Identifiers

CAS NUMBER:	106266-06-2
ATC CODE:	N05AX08
PubChem:	5073
DrugBank:	aprd00187
FORMULA:	$C_{23}H_{27}FN_4O_2$
MOL MASS:	410.485 g/mol
BIOAVAILABILITY:	70% oral
METABOLISM:	Hepatic (CYP2D6-mediated)
HALF-LIFE:	3–20 hours
EXCRETION:	Urinary

o

Duan Chengshi describes another type of (nonrecreational) medicine in the *Youyang zazu*:

Abosan comes from Syria. The tree is over one *zhang* tall, and its bark is greenish white... When one cuts the branches, there is a saplike oil which is used to apply to acariasis. There is nothing that it does not cure. The oil is exceedingly expensive and the value is greater than gold.

Fucking *fuck*. While we were bent over gathering cameras, Brunette Slut took the Zodiac. But to where? At this point she has enough gas to get halfway to one of the populated islands—if that. Ray offered the astute

Appearances are always deceiving in the biji, but none so much as when it comes to women. In Ji Yun's *Luan-yang xiaoxialu* ("Record of Spending the Summer at Luanyang"), a man named Er comes across a beautiful woman being attacked by a Daoist priest in the forest:

> The priest was going to slit open her heart, and the woman screamed for help. Er rode up to them at great speed and quickly held the priest by his hand. The woman gave off a loud cry, turned into a ray of light, and disappeared.
>
> The Daoist priest stamped his feet and said, "You've ruined it all! This demon has seduced and killed over a hundred people. That's why I caught her. I was going to kill her to eliminate this cause of trouble. Yet, because she has absorbed much human essence and gradually acquired spiritual powers over a period of time, her soul will escape if I simply cut off her head. So in order to kill her I have to slit open her heart. Now that you've released her, there will be endless trouble. This is to pity the life of a tiger and let it return to the deep mountains, not knowing how many deer in the swamps and forests will be devoured by it!"

observation that "It's always the brunette who stays under the radar for most of the game who wins these things, isn't it?" I had to agree.

So now it's me and him. On the steadicams we got to witness footage of what went down, *Blair Witch*–style: who killed whom and how. But that's another story, not mine.

In a nook in the rocks, I discovered six cans of Chinese tinned ham (or ham-like) product. Yes, it looked like pâté made from Jeffrey Dahmer's boyfriends, but to me it was a Sunday roast-beef lunch. I haven't shown Ray.

o

Maybe two hours after the Zodiac was pilfered, a fourteen-foot aluminum boat with Korean markings beached on the sand a few hundred yards down from us. Its sole passenger was a Korean fisherman. We're debating whether he has any foodstuffs onboard. Well, should he be unwilling to share, our flare guns and some heavy chunks of coral ought to be enough to do him in.

o

Here's the thing about survival: survival is merely survival. It's nothing else. It's not a work of art. It's only that you survived and someone else didn't.

NIVOLA

LIFE SPAN: 1914–1930 AD

NATURAL HABITAT: Spain

PRACTITIONER: Miguel de Unamuno

CHARACTERISTICS: Meandering, plotless, playful

Niebla ("Mist") was the first of several books that Miguel de Unamuno would call *nivolas*, a name invented in order to distinguish them from novels. The main difference between the nivola and the novel, as he saw it, was that a nivola has no plot, or rather that the plot is existential, and explicitly unknown to the author. In a nivola, the plot makes itself up as it goes along, put together by the characters themselves in a rebellion against their creator.

AN EXCERPT FROM

MIST

a nivola by MIGUEL DE UNAMUNO

—1914 AD—

Mist *follows the misadventures of Augusto Pérez, a young man confused about nearly everything in his life. In the novel, Augusto falls in love with at least two women, but since he doesn't trust his emotions or reality in general, his relationships with them are complicated. Fortunately, his trusty dog, Orfeo, is never too far away.*

HE SAT DOWN AGAIN, set her on his lap and enfolded her in his arms. He held her close to his chest. The sad creature raised an arm to his shoulder, as if to support herself on him, and again hid her head on his chest. Hearing his heart pound, she took fright.

"Do you feel all right, sir?"

"Whoever does?"

"Would you like me to order something for you?"

"No, no. I know what my trouble is! I must go on a trip." After a pause, he added: "Will you join me?"

"Don Augusto!"

"Leave off calling me 'Don'! Will you go with me or not?"

"As you wish…"

A mist clouded over Augusto's mind. His blood began to throb in his temples and he felt a pressure on his chest. To overcome it, he started to kiss Rosarito on her eyes, which she had to shut. Suddenly he stood up and said:

"Leave me! Leave me! I'm afraid!"

"Afraid of what?"

The girl's absolute composure unnerved him even further.

"I'm afraid. I don't know of whom. You, me, I don't know! Anybody! Maybe Liduvina! Listen, leave, go away! But you'll return, won't you?"

"Whenever you say."

"And you'll go with me on my trip, won't you?"

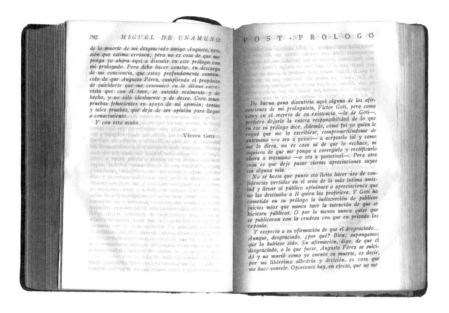

"Whatever you say…"

"Go away now!"

"And that woman…"

Augusto hurled himself at the young girl, who had stood up, seized her and pressed her against his chest. He put his dry lips to hers, and without actually kissing her, he held her for a spell, their mouths together. Suddenly he broke free and shook his head, and then, releasing her, he said:

"Get out! Go!"

Rosarito left immediately. Hardly was she out of the room, when Augusto, exhausted as if he had been running, threw himself on his bed, turned out the light and fell into a soliloquy:

I've been lying to her and to myself as well. It's always that way! Everything is phantasy, nothing but phantasy. As soon as a man speaks he lies, and if he talks to himself, that is, insofar as he is conscious that he thinks, he's lying to himself. The only truth lies in the physiological side of life, the physical. Speech is a social product and was created for the purpose of lying. I've heard a philosopher of ours say that truth is also a social product, something everyone believes in, and by believing in it, we finally come to understand each other. The real social product is the lie itself.

Suddenly, he felt his hand being licked, and he called out: "Oh, so you're here, Orfeo? Well, since you don't talk you don't tell lies, and I don't even think you're ever on the wrong track; you never even lie to yourself. But, since you're a domestic animal, some of the men's ways must have rubbed off on you… We men do nothing but lie and give ourselves airs. Words were invented for exaggerating our feelings and impressions—probably so we'd believe in them… words and speech and all the other conventional means of expressing ourselves, such as kissing, embracing… Every one of us does nothing but act out his role in life. We're all so many characters in a drama, mere masks, actors! No one really suffers or enjoys what he's saying or trying to express, but probably believes he is suffering or enjoying something. If it were not so, no one would be able to live. At heart we're all so passive. And so am I right now, playing out my drama as both actor and audience. The only pain that really kills is physical pain. The only truth is the physiological man, the man who doesn't speak, and so doesn't lie…"

He heard a knock at the door.

"What is it?"

"Aren't you going to have supper tonight?" Liduvina asked.

"Of course! I'll be there in a minute."

Translated by Warner Fite. Image from Miguel de Unamuno's Niebla.

SAVED

a new nivola by JOY WILLIAMS

CINNABAR'S MOTHER HAD summoned her.

"I'm giving the keynote address at an environmental conference. They're staging it at this swank resort. Hiking trails, seaweed wraps, four-hundred-thread-count sheets. Oxygen nutritional supplements, hydrogen-peroxide treatments—you ever hear of those?"

"Where are you?"

"You'll have to rent a car, it's true. Then you can drive me around to my obligations. I no longer have confidence in the drivers they provide. I don't know if you're aware of who David Halberstam was but David Halberstam's death marked the end of accepting courtesies from students in my book. Find a place that rents cars—you know how to do that, don't you? Call me back. I'll recite a series of numbers to them along with an expiration date and off you go."

"Okay," Cinnabar said. What a terrific opportunity, actually. To see her mother again under such unexpected and casual circumstances. Her mother had always told her she had a mind open to mirage.

"Call me Snow," her mother said. "That's what I go by, that's what everyone calls me now."

"I don't want to call you Snow."

"Well, don't be surprised when everyone else does."

Augusto, in *Mist*, on naming one's self: "In Homeric times people and things had two names: the name given them by man and the one given by the gods. I wonder what God calls me? And why shouldn't I call myself differently than I am called by other men?"

* * *

Snow's flight arrived on time. At the baggage claim, she noticed a young woman holding a sign: CHESTER OWEN CONFERENCE. Snow ignored her and went to a food station where she purchased a bottle of water. After a few swallows she threw the bottle away and it joined many more of its kind in a brimming trash receptacle. She looked at it blankly for several seconds, thinking of something else, while she shouldered the compact leather bag that contained all her needs for the three-day event. She was a respected eco-critic but did not consider herself, nor was she perceived to be, tiresome or predictable in her actions or beliefs.

She watched the greeter desperately waggling the sign as another clot of travelers floated down on the escalator. The girl snagged a balding man in a corduroy suit, and then another, this one bearded, defiantly careless in dirty jeans and a flannel shirt. Snow ambled up to them at last, having amused herself long enough by observing how doggedly they communicated with each other while awaiting her arrival, which of course had already occurred. As she approached, they were all agreeing how very much they admired the work of Chester Owen, who sadly would not be able to attend the very conference honoring him. He had taken a nasty spill and was confined to bed in his nineteenth-century farmhouse some distance away. A reception had been planned there for the last night of the conference but would have to be canceled. The farmhouse was fantastic and the Premarin foals Dr. Owen collected were fantastic too. They were Percherons—still babies but weighing thousands of pounds.

Snow feigned ignorance about Premarin foals.

"As I understand it," the bearded professor said, "they get this valuable hormone from the urine of pregnant mares but have no use for the resultant foal, which usually gets shipped off to the slaughterhouse. It's a big business. Owen has rescued at least a dozen of them but he'll never catch up to the reality of the numbers. Sweet old guy though."

The man had a peculiar odor. Was it his very breath? She drew back a little.

They were delayed when the balding man's luggage was claimed by another passenger, but Snow's colleague emerged victorious when the bag was unzipped to disclose numerous copies of a monograph he had written: *The Potentiality of Landscape's Emptiness: The Integrity of Half-Measures*. The losing claimant returned to the carousel in what seemed a state of fear.

Another scholar arrived, a former and devoted student of Chester

All action is frustrated in a nivola. Characters' best intentions result in failure or stasis. When Augusto, in *Mist*, announces to both of his love interests that he's about to take a long sojourn, it leads to an agonized interior monologue:

Would he take a trip or not? He had already announced it: first to Rosarito, without really knowing what he was saying, but just to say something, or more as a pretext for finding out if she'd join him, and then to Doña Ermelinda, to prove to her... What? What was he trying to prove by telling her he was about to go on a trip? Anything whatever! But now he had committed himself twice by having said he was going on a long trip. And he was a man of character himself, did he also have to prove that he was a man who kept his word?

Men who keep their word or promises first say one thing, then think about it and finally act on it, no matter how it works out. Men who keep their word neither deviate from or retract what they once said. And he, Augusto, had said he was going on a long, distant trip.

A long, distant trip! But why? What for? How and to where?

Owen. With him was his wife, a June, whose teeth had been dangerously over-whitened.

"I can't take you all," the greeter whose name was—Snow hadn't caught it actually—"I'd love to take you all but my car is, like, minuscule."

"I'm quite capable of getting there myself," Snow said.

"No, no," the greeter moaned.

"I'd rather," Snow said firmly.

The young woman was an associate professor specializing in the ecology of spring pools and on the long drive from the airport to the hotel in a vehicle which indeed was one of the smallest her passengers had ever experienced, proved herself to be an indifferent driver.

"I so apologize about the brakes," she said. "There's got to be something wrong with them."

Snow returned to the terminal and entered a bar, where she ordered water. It came in a large, elaborately crafted glass. The stem, though agonizingly twisted, was almost invisible, and she had to study the contraption before raising it to her lips.

She did not know Chester Owen. He was an expert on prairies, or had been; the field of study was ever expanding, concomitant with the natural grasslands' disappearance. It was easier to study something eradicated, to reconstruct it, not for future use or enjoyment but for knowledge, for the sake of knowledge. And now the old man, the distinguished honoree, whom she would never meet apparently, was rescuing Percherons, or were they Belgians, who would obliterate any meadow and whatever its precious grasses in an instant with their sinless, crushing jaws.

She gazed around her at the other patrons. Good God. But should we have stayed at home, wherever that might be... That was Elizabeth Bishop. She knew her Bishop. And no, we should not.

Tomorrow evening she would give her lecture but before that there would be a reception preceded by the papers and panels of others. Someone surely would bore them all by extolling that sanctimonious old pigeon, Thoreau, and his unimaginative trots into the Maine woods. She remembered that Cinnabar would not be arriving at all this night to escort her to the hotel. It would be tomorrow, tomorrow sometime that she would come. She sipped the water, which was maintaining its coldness in the innovative glass. But the glass was deceptive, too; suddenly there was nothing left.

Miguel de Unamuno's nivolas were mainly written in close third-person perspective, but they incorporated occasional glimpses of life beyond the main character. *Mist* focuses almost entirely on the thoughts and feelings of Augusto, but after one of his typically elliptical conversations, the story briefly follows another character instead:

> They parted company. When Doña Ermelinda arrived back home and recounted the conversation to her niece, Eugenia said to herself: "There's another woman. No doubt of it. Now I must have him."

Augusto says at one point, "We see how philosophy in great good part is pandering and pandering is philosophy."

* * *

Snow turned the heavy brass key, which for security and safety reasons had no number etched upon it, and entered her room. The liquid warbles of desert birds were playing softly on the radio. She could also detect the rolling rattle, the *quit quit quit* of the cowbird. One would certainly expect that to have been removed in production. Though perhaps realism was what they were after. Or was irony intended? Was realism always ironic?

The room was minimalist with touches of whimsy, the whimsy in Snow's case being a framed print of Rauschenberg's iconic angora-goat-and-tire combine, *Monogram*, upon the wall. A half-dozen purplish roses in a black vase were on the escritoire. The bedding was gray silk. There were three polished river stones on the coverlet that you were supposed to rub to relax or something. She'd been in places like this before. The wheatgrass and flax drink in the morning, the yoga mat, the Bose player, the bulbs that mimicked natural light whatever that was. In the bathroom were many small bottles of azure liquid, a label on each presenting an image of a rabbit with a line drawn through it and a statement that no creature had been harmed in the producing and testing of the product, an assurance that Snow found satisfaction in refuting by either the direct or indirect method when she had the energy. It wasn't long ago that rabbits perished by the thousands as human pregnancy indicators, she remembered. The rabbit died, congratulations. Isn't that what they said? But the rabbits always died, in fact.

She removed from her satchel the paper she would be delivering the next evening and placed it on the little desk with her notes. The unassimilated notes were always more intriguing than the finished product, but still she was pleased with the work, which she believed would restore viability to her field. On a fresh notecard she jotted down some thoughts on the goat. Perhaps *Monogram* could provide a monograph. The tire's essence could be traced to the rainforests of Brazil, which no longer existed. In countries like India and Brazil there was no conservation at all, or only as much as would not interfere with the living patterns of the people—*social ecology* it was called. Preserving biological diversity was impossible. She wrote quickly, the words becoming increasingly indecipherable. But it was important to get it down. She filled the fronts and backs of several cards in this manner before she turned off the light and sank down upon the bed.

Did you sleep well they would ask tomorrow. *Sleep well?*

She got up, took a long scarf from her bag, the favorite scarf she

---

In *Mist*, Augusto often vocally protests the omnipresence of little "realistic" details like this:

Daily detail! Give us today our daily bread! Give me, Lord, the endless detail of every day! The only reason we don't go under in the face of devastating sorrow or annihilating joy is because our sorrow and our joy are smothered in the thick fog of endless daily detail. All life is that: fog, mist. Life is a nebula.

Characters in *Mist* generally opt for the indirect method of refutation. At one point, Augusto and his close friend Victor Goti debate the existence of a philosopher famous for debating existence. Victor asks Augusto:

"What would you say is the greatest truth?"

"Well, one minute, now let's see… What Descartes said: 'I think, therefore I am.'"

"Not at all. The profoundest truth is that A = A."

"But that's nothing."

"That's exactly why it's the greatest of all truths, because it's nothing. But do you think that Descartes' twaddle is all that incontrovertible?"

"Just so…"

"Well then, did Descartes say it or didn't he?"

"Yes, of course he did!"

"Then, it is not true. For Descartes was never anything but a creature out of fiction, an invention of history, since… he neither existed… nor did he think, for that matter!"

"Who, then, uttered that famous statement?"

"No one at all said it. It was something said by itself."

always traveled with, and wrapped it around the Rauschenberg print. When it was securely veiled she returned to the cards and wrote: *Life is suffering. And death is suffering too.*

Then: *Critic (tk) says artist in these combines provides a form of redemption for luckless creature, a modest resurrection.*

Then, over this last, for there was no more space: *Absurd!!*

Snow opened her eyes to the pulsating red nipple of the message light. The scarf she had placed over the Rauschenberg fluttered in the thin wash of cooling air from the duct overhead. It was as though the wretched goat in his unyielding circle of tire was attempting to be alive, breathing in and out.

When she rang the desk she was told by a pleasant voice that she was being moved to other lodgings, in the same resort complex of course. There was a pharmaceutical convention arriving that evening—there had been an error in blocking out the reservations.

"Is everyone in my group being moved? We eco-critics?" she added wryly.

"Yes," the pleasant voice said. "If you could be ready no later than noon, that would be super."

She replaced the receiver but the light continued to pulse. She called the desk again.

"Are there any more messages?"

She was told there were not but that it took a few moments for the switchboard system to reset.

But the light continued to pulse even after Snow had bathed and dressed.

In the lobby, many of the conferees had gathered around a large, brightly lit aquarium. Even the elaborate grottoes through which the fish swam in a mechanical fashion offered no shadow.

Snow said to no one in particular, "Darwin initially thought fish designed their own eyes."

"Gosh," someone said, "that fits right in with the talk I'll be giving after lunch. It has to do with our perception. I am really concerned with our ability to perceive."

"Cabot's still working on his paper," June, the student's wife, said. "He owes his career, for what it is, to Chester Owen and is just beloved by the man but I tell him, sure, honey, do your best but don't give yourself an ulcer, Chester Owen won't even be in attendance and Cabot argues all the more reason the paper has to be perfect in every way and I tell him, look, I know these people, I've had the same experience with

In his (fictional) prologue to *Mist*, Augusto's friend Victor describes "Don Miguel's" (Unamuno's) fascination with the buffo-tragic, "tragic farce or farcical tragedy," in which aspects of the grotesque and the farcical are not just intertwined but fused together.

Unamuno's characters regularly announce themselves with lofty thematic preferences. The uncle of Augusto's beloved Eugenia tells him:

"Yes, dear sir, I am an anarchist, a mystical anarchist. A theoretical anarchist only, of course; you understand, a theoretical anarchist. Never fear, friend," and he rested a hand gently on Augusto's knee. "I throw no bombs. My anarchism is purely spiritual. After all, my friend, I have my own ideas about practically everything…"

these people as you have, and if they hear even a quarter of what you have to tell them, it'll be a miracle.

"We visited the Doctor earlier this morning," she went on. "We brought orange juice and pastries which he didn't touch so we brought them back but we saw him and those huge horses. They were everywhere, two of them even stuck their big heads into the sickroom. He keeps the window open so they can do that. I don't know how he manages the flies but he manages them somehow, there were very few, but he's not long for this world in my opinion, poor guy."

"What do you mean?" Snow asked. "Not long for this world…"

"Doesn't everybody—" June began.

"'Body my house my horse my hound what will I do when you are fallen when Body my good bright dog is dead…'" someone recited in a plummy voice.

"Elizabeth Bishop?" the balding man ventured.

Snow winced and gently probed her temples.

"No. Same generation, though. M—"

"Really? It sounds so… so archaic."

You couldn't just be simple and friendly with these people, June thought. They wanted to eat you alive.

The receptionist approached the group. "Now everything's been taken care of, your luggage has been sent ahead," she of the agreeable voice assured them. She wore a stylishly cut suit and her hair was streaked with azure in complement with the color scheme of the public rooms.

With the others, Snow attended a panel in which the word *viewshed* was used with abandon. This was followed by an exhibition of photographs taken by the head of the earth-sciences department at the nearby institute of higher learning. The photographs depicted holes of various kinds, shot with sophistication and sorrowful celebration in black and white.

Then there was luncheon. There was one incident. When asked if she had previously met a respected urban wildlife biologist, Snow replied that she had only had the horror of a brief acquaintance. This was pronounced "screamingly funny" by a poet who had earlier been described as someone who took extraordinary risks in her work, and what could have been an awkward moment passed.

Snow begged off the afternoon panels and, following an elaborate set of directions provided by the poet, walked through a managed, sustainably responsible wood toward her new lodging, which turned out to be a featureless structure rising aggressively and inorganically from a mottled plain. Pink golf carts encircled it.

Victor, in *Mist*, finds high-flown language grating. "The more profound a phrase, the emptier it is," he says. "There is nothing more profound than a bottomless well."

A more effective strategy is suggested by Victor:

The man who devours, enjoys himself, but he can't help thinking of the end of all his pleasure, and that turns him into a pessimist; the man who is devoured suffers, and he can't help looking forward to the end of his suffering, and so he becomes an optimist. So devour yourself, and since the pleasure of devouring yourself will be confused with the pain of being devoured, one neutralizing the other, you'll achieve a perfect equanimity of spirit, in other words, ataraxia. Then you'll be merely a spectacle for yourself.

Unamuno's ideal luncheon joke would be more disruptive. In *Mist*'s introduction, Goti writes,

Don Miguel insists that if the point is to make people laugh, it should not be a matter of helping them to contract their diaphragms for easier digestion, but rather to provoke their vomiting whatever they have gobbled down. The meaning of life and of the universe can be more clearly seen on an empty stomach— without sweetmeats or banquets.

In the lobby were tall potted palms with fraying, yellowing fronds. They looked realistically unhealthy but were probably fake. Before a fireplace of unlit logs there was a table with a bowl of wrapped candies and an untidy stack of newspapers. At the desk, a manager who offered that he had never heard of Chester Owen provided her with a key of slim plastic perforated with holes.

It engaged with the lock on her door with a sullen click. Her bag had preceded her and was placed above the gaping dark screen of a television set, the centerpiece of the austere room. A plate, covered in foil, with eating utensils tucked into a folded napkin, was atop the bag. It was undoubtedly the remains of her wearisome lunch, which she had certainly not requested.

Sliding the coarse curtains to one side, she raised the window, something she had never bothered to do at the Azure. The room looked out onto a narrow shaft that terminated many stories below in an immaculate alley.

She picked up the plate—what unmemorable thing had she ordered anyway?—and turned back the foil. It was scraps, wide circlets of fat, cubed pieces of pale meat, skeins of puckered skin. She gasped, then flung it through the open window.

In the lobby, she sat at the cluttered table, reviewing the notes for her talk and yawning.

"Do you know what day it is?" a woman's voice inquired.

"Yes," Snow said, annoyed.

"My Marie would have been twenty-seven years of age today. This is her day attendant come round once more." The woman tapped the top paper of a disheveled pile with a not-very-clean finger. It was the obituary page and the finger was directing her to a black-bordered memorium of a child in a sunsuit holding a book upside down. Having noticed the inverted book first and the blond-ringletted child only later, Snow felt at an immediate disadvantage in the situation.

"Two," the woman said.

"I'm sorry."

"Only two. I've been doing this for twenty-five years now and I'll be doing it for twenty-five more if I've got the breath."

Poor little creature, Snow thought, placed on the poor altar of brief appraisals, the brief appraisals of strangers, year after year.

"It's working out pretty well."

By this lunatic, Snow thought.

"Lots of people know her now, over the years. Hundreds. She's not

In his short story "Saint Emmanuel The Good, Martyr," one of his last works of fiction, Unamuno's main character, a parish priest who no longer believes in god, argues for the importance of feigning faith in situations like this:

I am here to make the souls of my parishioners live, to make them happy and to make them dream themselves immortal, and not to kill them. What is needed here is that they live in a healthy way in unanimity of feeling, and with the truth, with my truth, they wouldn't live. Let them live... True religion? All religions are true insofar as they make their people that profess them live spiritually, insofar as they console them for having been born to die, and for each people the truest religion is theirs, the one that has made them. And mine? Mine is to console myself by consoling others, although the consolation I give them is not mine.

so shy anymore. She used to be wicked shy. She didn't like to have her picture took."

"So sorry," Snow managed.

"Imagine her a little. Like what would she be doing right now."

"But I cannot," Snow said simply.

"What would it cost you to imagine this child?"

The woman was rocking back and forth in her chair and seemed to be revolving slightly at the same time.

"It's a big help to Marie," she cried. "Marie appreciates it. Marie wouldn't be nothing without your help."

"She's drinking tea," Snow said hurriedly, "enjoying a moment by herself."

The woman frowned. "Why would she want to be by herself?"

"She's in a garden, one of those beautiful seaside gardens which she designed herself down to the smallest detail. She's planting bulbs."

"Too late in the year for bulbs," the woman said, her frown deepening.

A familiar face swam into view, that of the ecology-of-spring-pools person.

"Ready for the big event?" she chirped to Snow.

"What did it cost you? It didn't cost you nothing, did it?" The woman slumped in her chair and stared poisonously at both of them.

Snow gratefully accepted a ride from the ecology-of-spring-pools person. She was not technically violating the student-driver rule for the girl was an adjunct professor.

"What is your name again, dear?"

"Lucy."

"Lucy. Lucy? Like juicy?"

"Ugh, I hope not," the girl laughed, though that had been a problem of agonizing proportions in the cruelty of the schoolyard years before. But she had outgrown, outpaced, those brats, those dicks, those turds, long, long ago. She shook her head and blinked rapidly. "It's a pity you missed the panel on the egoism of perception," she said. "It became quite scrappy. E. H. Klamm argued that wilderness can exist comfortably in our cities and suburbs while Cabot Smith said that he wants a wilderness from which civilization must avert its glance." Lucy saw herself biting her tormentors, trying not to cry. Juicy Lucy, circling like an animal tied to a post. Still:

"Those are someone else's words, I believe," Snow said.

Unamuno was fascinated by the ability of art and imagination to extend life beyond what is allowed by science. In *Abel Sanchez*, another of his nivolas, the two main characters are Abel, a painter, and Joaquín Monegro, his envious doctor friend. Joaquín discusses one incident in which their talents collided:

I was attending a poor woman, who was rather dangerously, but still not desperately, ill. Abel had made a portrait of her; a magnificent portrait, one of his best, one of those which have remained as definitive among his works. And it was this painting which was this first thing that came into my sight—and into my hate—as soon as I entered the sick woman's home. In the portrait she was alive, more alive than in her bed of suffering flesh and bone. And the portrait seemed to say to me: Look, he has given me life forever! Let's see if you can prolong this other, earthly life of mine! At the bedside of the poor invalid, as I listened to her heart and took her pulse, I was obsessed by the other woman, the painted one. I was stupefied, completely stupefied, and as a result the poor woman died on me; or rather, I let her die... The portrait looked at me, regardless of whether or not I looked at it, and it drew my gaze perforce... I let her die, and he resurrected her.

Augusto, in *Mist*, shares this sentiment: "Usage breaks down all beauty, destroys it. The noblest role of any object is that of being contemplated. How beautiful an orange still uneaten!"

"Pardon?"

"'Wanting a wilderness from which civilization would avert its glance.' I believe those are someone else's words." Though whose, exactly, escaped Snow. Loving the dead was like wanting that wilderness. It was quite desirable and unreasonable. Even so, the confusion that loving the dead always elicited in her vanished for a moment.

"Shall we go," Lucy said glumly.

Some poet, not the one who took extraordinary risks, was speaking about living in the now, about the necessity to frankly celebrate the fearful flux that is nature.

"If you have to live in the now, where were you living in the then?" Snow whispered to Lucy, who was seated beside her in the lecture hall.

Lucy stifled a whimper.

A member of the audience stood and was given a battery-operated microphone.

"I was peeling an orange this morning," she said silently.

She jabbed at the side of the instrument with her thumb.

"I was peeling an orange this morning," she said, "and I noticed that the peel I was about to throw into the garbage reminded me of squamous cells, those tiny epidermal flakes that fall from our skin. I then realized without knowing it that we are all… all sowers who spread tiny particles of skin here and there along our path. We create with our very waste."

"Interesting," the poet said.

The bearded man, wearing the same soiled jeans and flannel shirt he'd arrived in, rose. The microphone was reluctantly surrendered to him.

"I have a question," he said. "Isn't it all about boundaries, the crossing and assimilation of boundaries?"

"The elimination of boundaries," the poet said, "and their assimilation. Yes, that's an excellent question."

Snow raised her hands to her head and gently probed her temples. She felt like a heated stove. And someone was flicking water on the stove to hear it snap. She had done this as a child and been severely reprimanded when observed.

"I must get some air," she whispered to Lucy. She wove her way upward through the dimness, occasionally veering into an unoccupied seat. "Sorry," she said. "Excuse me. So sorry." She pushed open a door that seemed remarkably heavy—at first she thought it was locked—and gained the hallway where tables had been set. There were cardboard

Augusto tells his friend Victor a story of unreasonable love, and forcibly averted glances, in *Mist*:

In a small Portuguese village there was a pyrotechnician or fogueteiro, as they say there, whose wife was a stunning creature… he delighted in making the rest of mankind's mouth water, so to speak, and he showed her off, as if to say, "Do you see this woman? Does she appeal to you? Well, she's mine and nobody else's!"… On one occasion when he was preparing a [fireworks] display, with his gorgeous wife at his side for inspiration, the powder caught fire and there was an explosion. Both husband and wife were carried out unconscious, and both were seriously burned. A large part of his wife's face was affected, as well as her breast, and she was left hideously disfigured. Luckily, the fogueteiro was completely blinded by the accident, so that he never saw his wife's terrible disfigurement. And he continued to be as proud as ever of his wife's beauty, raving to one and all.

In *Mist*, Augusto eventually comes around to the value of boredom:

Yes, there is such a thing as unconscious tedium. Most of us, nearly all of us, are unconsciously bored. Tedium is the substrate of life, and it is from tedium that most games have been invented, games and novels—and love. Life's mist distills a bittersweet liquor which is tedium.

cartons that had spigots jammed into them and that, in her unhappy experience, contained searingly hot and tasteless coffee. There were sweets and strawberries. There was also wine, thank god.

"White," she said. But there was no one to pour it, and the bottles had yet to be uncorked.

The doors to the lecture hall were flung open. There was a great surging of applause. They were applauding the absent guest of honor who was curled in the distance on his bed, attended with immense unconcern by the horses he had saved. She should have gone out there with the toothy June and her devout, unoriginal husband. Oh how she wished she had done so! She would have slipped into the poor old man's bed and embraced his poor old man's body, fitting his hesitant, irregular breathing to her own. He would smell of withered prairies, his eyes would be a fading wildflower blue. Everything he had worked for had been lost. She would reassure him in his belief that each of us is meant to rescue the world and she would wean him from his affinities to that world as one would wean a baby from the mother's milk.

"There you are," Lucy said, squeezing her arm rather painfully and ushering her back into the lecture hall to fulfill her obligations there.

Augusto has similar fantasies:

To sleep together, not just lying alongside each other while each one dreams his own separate dream, but really to sleep together, both in the same dream!… This cursed business of sleeping alone, alone with a single, lone dream! The dream of one person alone is mere illusion, a mere appearance. The dream of a couple is a true dream, a reality.

"Thank god that's over," Snow said to an uncommunicative geographer who was returning her to her hotel. He had never heard of Chester Owen but was fulfilling some of the duties his scholarship required by being, as he put it, on hand.

"Yeah," he said.

"I'm waiting on someone though so I'm staying on a bit."

"Yeah. Cool," he said.

Snow was swept upward efficiently in the malodorous elevator but the strip of plastic no longer offered entry to her room. She returned vexed and weary to the lobby. The newspapers had been cleared from the table and the floors were wet from mopping. The desk clerk was staring at her, rather insolently, she thought. Could someone possibly have witnessed her earlier desecration of their immaculate alley? Or perhaps that woman who had accosted her was a palace pet, someone whom she had treated carelessly at her own peril. Perhaps there were long-standing rules of engagement and modes of deference that Snow had ignored, though of course she would have had no idea what they were.

The clerk was gesturing to her, waving her over. Perhaps someone had made a complaint? Or they were moving her again?

"Tell me," he said, and his tone really was unmistakably hostile, "why do you believe that everything's been taken care of?"

The numbers didn't add up. There were two too many. The code wasn't valid.

Still, Cinnabar moved toward the east on a highway that grew exceedingly wider.

"The open road," the third trucker said.

A dog ran across the highway, four lanes, five, seven... There was jeering, honking, laughing cries of support. He gained the median and paused before assaying the next three lanes, five, six.

"He'll be the first my god in my experience on this fucking route," the driver said.

No one had named the dog but his name was Orfeo.

Orfeo.

If you chanced to call him that, he would come to you still.

Ambiguous endings are central to the nivola. Unamuno wrote that "I have no reason to satisfy your frivolous, serial-story curiosity. Every reader who in reading a novel worries about how the characters will finish without worrying about how he will finish does not deserve to have his curiosity satisfied."

Mist ends with an epilogue supposedly written by the protagonist's dog, Orfeo.

SENRYŪ

LIFE SPAN: 1765 AD–present

NATURAL HABITAT: Japan

PRACTITIONERS: Senryū Karai, Shūji Terayama

CHARACTERISTICS: Brief, cynical, humorous

Senryū are short, unrhymed poems similar to haiku: three lines long, and made up of no more than seventeen syllables altogether. Generally, senryū address human nature—relationships, work, war—while haiku focus on the phenomena of the physical world.

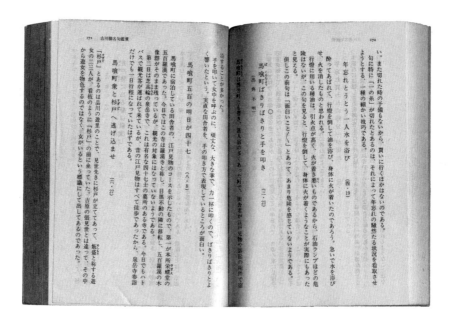

Senryū emerged as an offshoot of haiku during eighteenth-century Edo-period Japan. They were given their name—which means "river willow"—by Karai Hachiemon, sometime around 1740. Karai eventually adopted "Karai Senryū" as his pen name, although he did not write many senryū himself. (He did assemble several anthologies devoted to the form, and presided over senryū contests. According to Haruo Shirane, editor of Early Modern Japanese Literature, Karai is "known primarily as a judge rather than a poet.") After Karai's death, successive figureheads of the senryū "school" adopted his pen name as their own, but senryū themselves were almost always authored anonymously.

UNTITLED SENRYŪ

authors unknown

When the night falls
the day starts to break
on the brothels

> *—Translated by Makoto Ueda.*
> *From* Yanagidaru shūi, *vol. 6 (c. 1796), edited by Karai Senryū.*

His wife away from home
he spends the entire day
looking for things

> *—Translated by Makoto Ueda.*
> *From* Kawazoi Yanagi, *vol. 5 (c. 1780), edited by Akera Kankō.*

Laying a fart—
no humor in it
when you live alone

> *—Translated by Burton Watson.*
> *From* Yanagidaru, *vol. 3 (c. 1768), edited by Karai Senryū.*

The official's little son—
how fast he's learned to open
and close his fist!

> *—Translated by Makoto Ueda.*
> *From* Yanagidaru, *vol. 1 (1765), edited by Karai Senryū.*

"There'll soon be
a charming widow"—that's the talk
among the doctors

> *—Translated by Makoto Ueda.*
> *From* Yanagidaru, *vol. 5 (c. 1770), edited by Karai Senryū.*

NEW SENRYŪ

After ten years, I wrote him: "Now?"
He returned the word,
one letter gone.

>   *—Nicky Beer*

Filleting a fish
He shows us the skeleton
As though he made it

>   *—Dan Liebert*

At his father's wake: "He looks good.
Real good." Then he shrugs,
"Pretty good."

>   *—Douglas W. Milliken*

Find for tender strong man
For make babies, cook
Love, Natasha (view pics)

>   *—Byron Lu*

Lab results came back
Seems that I'm an alien.
Are you and dad too?

>   *—Chris Spurr*

SOCRATIC DIALOGUE

LIFE SPAN: 399–51 BC

NATURAL HABITAT: Greece, Rome

PRACTITIONERS: Plato, Xenophon, Antisthenes, Alexamenes
of Teos, Theocritus, Tissaphernes, Aristotle, Cicero

CHARACTERISTICS: Didactic, pensive, philological, moralistic

A Socratic dialogue follows the philosophical back-and-forth between
a learned elder and his (or her) students, dramatizing political, social,
moral, and existential issues through a confrontational dialectic.
Dialogues often have narrative aspects, and some incorporate small talk.
Xenophon's *Symposium* sets the conversation at a dinner party, and features an argument between Socrates and Lycon over proper hygiene.

AN EXCERPT FROM THE

REPUBLIC

a Socratic dialogue by PLATO

—c. 380 bc—

Plato's Republic *follows Socrates's conversation with several interlocutors—Glaucon and Adeimantus, primarily—as they discuss the ideal state, the role of art, and the nature of the just. The dialogue takes place at the home of a philosopher named Polemarchus, in Piraeus.*

SOCRATES: Listen then, or rather let me ask you a question. Can you tell me what is meant by representation in general? I have no very clear notion myself.

GLAUCON: So you expect me to have one!

SOCRATES: Why not? It is not always the keenest eye that is the first to see something.

GLAUCON: True; but when you are there I should not be very desirous to tell what I saw, however plainly. You must use your own eyes.

SOCRATES: Well then, shall we proceed as usual and begin by assuming the existence of a single essential nature or Form for every set of things which we call by the same name? Do you understand?

GLAUCON: I do.

SOCRATES: Then let us take any set of things you choose. For instance there are any number of beds or of tables, but only two Forms, one of Bed and one of Table.

GLAUCON: Yes.

SOCRATES: And we are in the habit of saying that the craftsman, when he makes the beds or tables we use or whatever it may be, has before his mind the Form of one or other of these pieces of furniture. The Form itself is, of course, not the work of any craftsman. How could it be?

GLAUCON: It could not.

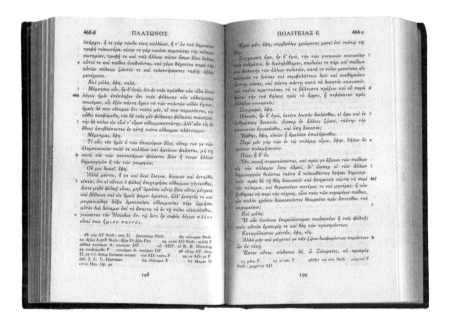

SOCRATES: Now what name would you give to a craftsman who can produce all the things made by every sort of workman?

GLAUCON: He would need to have very remarkable powers!

SOCRATES: Wait a moment, and you will have even better reason to say so. For, besides producing any kind of artificial thing, this same craftsman can create all plants and animals, himself included, and earth and sky and gods and the heavenly bodies and all the things under the earth in Hades.

GLAUCON: That sounds like a miraculous feat of virtuosity.

SOCRATES: Are you incredulous? Tell me, do you think there could be no such craftsman at all, or that there might be someone who could create all these things in one sense, though not in another? Do you not see that you could do it yourself, in a way?

GLAUCON: In what way, I should like to know.

SOCRATES: There is no difficulty; in fact there are several ways in which the thing can be done quite quickly. The quickest perhaps would be to take a mirror and turn it round in all directions. In a very short time you could produce sun and stars and earth and yourself and all the other animals and plants and lifeless objects which we mentioned just now.

GLAUCON: Yes, in appearance, but not the actual things.

SOCRATES: Quite so; you are helping out my argument. My notion is that a painter is a craftsman of that kind. You may say that the things he produces are not real; but there is a sense in which he too does produce a bed.

Translated by Francis MacDonald Cornford. Image from Plato's Republic.

AFTER CITIZEN KANE

a new Socratic dialogue by DAVID THOMSON

THE SCENE IS A *civilized urban square in the world to come, with a coffeehouse—more newspapers and chess than Madeleine Peyroux—strangely but conveniently inhabited by people we have already known: this day, the well-trained celebrity hound might recognize Franz Kafka, sipping at an endless espresso; Virginia Woolf, warming her chilled hands on a nonfat latte; Ernest Hemingway, whose beer glass of filtered coffee—made with the clearest springwater taken in the early morning from a shaded northern Spanish stream—might well be spiked with grappa (the good grappa); and Charles Chaplin, who has settled for a restoring cup of English breakfast tea. They are broken in on by a newcomer, a welcome visitor—a tall, dark woman with a flash of steel in her hair. It is Susan Sontag, and she is agitated.*

SONTAG: I'll be damned if I'm going along with it! It's a caving-in! There's no serious intellectual responsibility anymore!

KAFKA [*Looking up with interest*]: Oh, good—gossip. What can this be?

CHAPLIN: At last! I was beginning to think nothing happened up here.

HEMINGWAY: Don't you worry, Mr. C.—it's when nothing happens here that you can feel life stirring, like a trout under the far bank of the stream. You have to wait and keep yourself very still—

Socratic dialogues were often set in locales considered amenable to intellectual discussion. Xenophon's *Symposium* dinner-party debate is arranged after Callias, encountering Socrates outside of the racetrack, tells him,

> This is an opportune meeting, for I am about to give a dinner in honour of Autolycus and his father; and I think that my entertainment would present a great deal more brilliance if my dining-room were graced with the presence of men like you, whose hearts have undergone philosophy's purification, than it would with generals and cavalry commanders and office-seekers.

WOOLF [*Groaning*]: Oh, please, Papa—enough of the fisherman act! Everyone can do it now. It's just a stale trick.

SONTAG: Enough, children. Listen to what I say. Last night—absolutely in the spirit of duty, I went to see it again.

WOOLF: What did you see, dear? It seems to have got you excited.

SONTAG: No, it didn't, and there's my point exactly. It didn't reach me. Of course, I know it inside out. But there are people who promise you you'll see something fresh every time you see it, that it's a gift that keeps on giving. Well, I looked again—I thought I should in view of the vote.

KAFKA: What vote is that? You know, I have never voted.

SONTAG: 2012.

CHAPLIN: Heavens! That's too far away to think about.

WOOLF: It'll come soon enough.

SONTAG: Exactly! And if some of us don't start thinking about it in time—well, for all we know, the same old chestnut will win again.

WOOLF: Do you mean the Oscars? I thought everyone had agreed they were a foolishness.

SONTAG: No, not the Oscars, Auntie. In 2012, *Sight & Sound*, the British film magazine, will once again call on filmmakers and critics to vote for the ten best films ever made.

KAFKA: How vulgar.

SONTAG: Franz, we know it's vulgar. We are all au fait with vulgarity, don't you worry your anxious eyes about that. But intellectuals have to stand up for that special place—that voice, that echo of meaning—that they may occupy in society.

WOOLF: I always vote on *American Idol*. [*Despairing laughter from the others.*] I do. I think it's charming. That show can cheer me up sometimes better than a Cornish cream tea.

KAFKA: What I meant was calling a film magazine *Sight & Sound* instead

Participants in the dialogues often chided and kidded each other, particularly when it seemed as if someone was taking himself too seriously.

In Plato's *Republic*, Socrates suggests that, in an ideal society, the best intellectuals would serve as philosopher kings.

of something like *Kiss, Kiss, Bang, Bang* or *Virtual Coming. Sight &
Sound* is so academe and intimidating—it's so *Cahiers du Cinéma*. It
makes you wonder if you're deaf and blind.

CHAPLIN: Kafka, my dear fellow, you didn't live long enough to witness
the greatest vulgarity—sound! Just one of the countless things
that have killed the movies.

KAFKA: Charlie, I died early enough to be a ghost, and I can tell you
that apart from the Jewish race, the idea of beauty, and the vitality
of language, nothing has more funerals than the movies. So ghosts
understand them very well. And a lot of people told me I was a
ghost long before I had my death papers.

WOOLF: I think so often, my boys, it's the precondition that lets one live
after one's date with the River Ouse, if you know what I mean.

HEMINGWAY: He that took responsibility for his own departure, he has
begun his afterlife.

WOOLF: If you don't mind, really, I think that's in revolting taste. My
suicide came from an unbearable anguish in the soul.

HEMINGWAY: And mine was public relations?

WOOLF: My dear Papa, you are rather the poet of the Cooperman
catalogue, if you know what I mean—all cryptic sentences and
bias-cut clothes.

SONTAG: Could we have a little order? This is a debate and it deserves
a subject. We are talking about the cinema and its possible
greatness. Last night, I went back to see *Citizen Kane*.

CHAPLIN: Don't tell me: you saw it on your computer.

SONTAG: Charlie, give me some credit. I made movies, too, you know—

KAFKA [*Whispers*]: Don't get caught in the dark with them!

SONTAG: I know, I know, but I am not making huge claims. Let's
agree I have believed in beauty and tried to find it through the
viewfinder. So give me credit for treating *Kane* properly. They ran
it for me last night at the Heavenly in one of the best old nitrate
35 mm prints. It felt so moist I believed I could swim in it.

Socrates was executed by the state
of Athens; unlike Kafka, he had no
written work to survive him. The
classical Socratic dialogues were
dramatized portrayals of his teach-
ings, written by his pupils and con-
temporaries rather than by Socrates
himself.

WOOLF: I read somewhere that to see *Kane* alone was the perfect equation of megalomania.

SONTAG: I think that's right, because I believe that young Mr. Welles was quite deliberately setting out to make the greatest picture ever made.

CHAPLIN: He wanted to make a picture that might be the first ever made—and the last!

HEMINGWAY: I've known bullfighters like that. All elegance and pride. They ended up with a horn in their crutch.

KAFKA: Perfection should always be accidental. Or incidental.

SONTAG: There's the point. *Sight & Sound* has been doing these polls every ten years since 1952. *Citizen Kane* came first in 1962—and it's been first every decade since.

CHAPLIN: Aha, what won in '52?

SONTAG: First place went to *Bicycle Thieves*.

CHAPLIN [*Cast down*]: Oh!

SONTAG: But I must tell you that in second place, my dear Sir Charlie, was something called *City Lights*.

KAFKA: A film that depends on a blind character, if you recall.

CHAPLIN: Ah, yes, *City Lights*—what a time of my life. Days in a row, you know, the whole crew and the cast just waited for me to be inspired.

HEMINGWAY: How in hell did you pay for that?

CHAPLIN: My own money, old boy, the only way to go.

KAFKA: There's the riddle. In 1920, it's a man or a woman and a sheet of paper. They find the story and the words on their own. But for a movie you need a million dollars and how can anyone get a million dollars without destroying their artistic souls?

HEMINGWAY: So every movie there ever was is some kind of shit? It's a compromise?

SONTAG: But, Papa, last week at the Heavenly, they played *To Have and Have Not*—

Results of the 1952 *Sight & Sound* Critics' Poll to determine the best films of all time:

1. *Bicycle Thieves*
2. *City Lights*
   The Gold Rush (tie)
4. *Battleship Potemkin*
5. *Intolerance*
   Louisiana Story (tie)
7. *Greed*
   Le Jour se lève
   The Passion of Joan of Arc (tie)
10. *Brief Encounter*
    Le Million
    La Règle du jeu (tie)

Plato's *Republic* also comments on the vexed relationship between money and one's soul. While discussing inheritance with Cephalus, Socrates says,

I see that you are indifferent about money, which is a characteristic rather of those who have inherited their fortunes than of those who have acquired them; the makers of fortunes have a second love of money as a creation of their own, resembling the affection of authors for their own poems, or of parents for their children, besides that natural love of it for the sake of use and profit which is common to them and all men. And hence they are very bad company, for they can talk about nothing but the praises of wealth.

KAFKA: Perfect ghost story.

WOOLF: It is, isn't it!

SONTAG: And it was packed. I saw it and the audience was reciting the words along with the characters onscreen.

HEMINGWAY: "You do know how to whistle, don't you?" I never wrote a damn word of that.

CHAPLIN: But the public doesn't know. *To Have and Have Not* is one of our classic pictures. You got paid for it—and then look at the royalties.

KAFKA: It's a good book, too. And a good film.

SONTAG: But never the twain shall meet.

WOOLF: Why should they? I don't expect movies to be grand and solemn. I prefer them to stay silly.

CHAPLIN: People used to say I was effortlessly foolish.

HEMINGWAY: And naturally stupid.

SONTAG: But stupid is not the same as silly.

KAFKA: By no means—don't you think that certain kinds of ballet dancing can be so solemn, you want to laugh? You want him to drop her. You long for the tragic error. But then take Mr. Astaire—

WOOLF: Oh, I love Fred.

KAFKA: And he is—don't you see—authentically insignificant, or very light. Like zabaglione.

SONTAG: But Astaire is a very great artist, surely?

KAFKA: No, I think he is a very light artist. I mean, *Top Hat*, *Swing Time*, *Funny Face*, *Silk Stockings*—take your pick. No one could say any of those films is "about" anything—except they are excuses for being Fred Astaire movies.

HEMINGWAY: But Astaire always plays the kind of guy if you bumped into him in life you'd say, That's a very thin fellow. There's not much substance there. He's like a fragrance in hard shoes.

The effect of the original Socratic dialogues also depended to some extent on the involvement of a crowd of spectators. Socratic debates and discussions were held in the gymnasium in ancient Athens, with onlookers interrupting and asking questions.

The question of taste, and how much weight it should be given, is raised in a famously deleted scene from Stanley Kubrick's film *Spartacus* portraying Crassus's attempted seduction of his servant, Antoninus. The exchange was structured by the screenwriter, Dalton Trumbo, as a Socratic dialogue:

CRASSUS: Do you steal, Antoninus?
ANTONINUS: No, master.
CRASSUS: Do you lie?
ANTONINUS: Not if I can avoid it.
CRASSUS: Have you ever dishonored the gods?
ANTONINUS: No, master.
CRASSUS: Do you refrain from these vices out of respect for the moral virtues?
ANTONINUS: Yes, master.
CRASSUS: Do you eat oysters?
ANTONINUS: When I have them, master.
CRASSUS: Do you eat snails?
ANTONINUS: No, master.
CRASSUS: Do you consider the eating of oysters to be moral and the eating of snails to be immoral?
ANTONINUS: No, master.
CRASSUS: Of course not. It is all a matter of taste, isn't it?
ANTONINUS: Yes, master.
CRASSUS: And taste is not the same as appetite... and therefore not a question of morals, is it?
ANTONINUS: It could be argued so, master.
CRASSUS: That will do. My robe, Antoninus. My taste includes both snails and oysters.

SONTAG: But is he actually silly—without intellectual weight—or does his grace just rise above any question of meaning?

KAFKA: You could never mistake him for Hamlet. Or Quentin Compson. But it may be better in life not to be them—don't be a tragic character, just learn to dance. And then everyone feels better watching you.

SONTAG: You mean a musical might be the greatest film ever made.

CHAPLIN: W. C. Fields once said that I was really a ballet dancer.

Fields said of Chaplin that "the son of a bitch is a ballet dancer. He's the best ballet dancer that ever lived and if I get a chance, I'll strangle him with my bare hands."

HEMINGWAY: Or the best picture could be a Fields film—did you ever see a finer portrait of man's tortured life, trying to steer a way between women and drink without stooping to murder? People laugh at Bill Fields, but he's the true voice of desperation.

WOOLF: Yet somehow we think that if we are laughing, the subject cannot be serious.

CHAPLIN: There you are! The great comics are the most serious people. Look at that Chip Allen.

SONTAG: Woody Allen!

CHAPLIN: Of course.

WOOLF: But when he puts on a Swedish accent, he's quite dire, don't you think?

SONTAG: And nowhere near as funny as Bergman.

KAFKA: But the great clowns do very badly on prize day.

CHAPLIN: Thank you for saying that. Do you know they never gave me an Oscar—not until I was dying.

In Plato's *Ion*, Socrates's interlocutor is a prizewinning actor (Ion) who shares this sentiment. "If I set [the audience] crying," he says, "I shall laugh myself because of the money I take, but if they laugh, I myself shall cry because of the money I lose." Socrates, unsympathetic and generally skeptical of the idea that acting deserves any recognition at all, later says, "You are only a deceiver, and so far from exhibiting the art of which you are a master, will not, even after my repeated entreaties, explain to me the nature of it."

KAFKA: In America it is always advantageous to be close to death. There are no Oscars either for Buster Keaton, the Marx Brothers, Fields, Laurel and Hardy, or Jerry Lewis.

SONTAG: But why do we vote for *Kane*? Is it habit?

WOOLF: That young Mr. Welles knew how to take himself seriously. We followed suit like lambs. And it's a film about America—

Americans always fall for that.

CHAPLIN: They think they invented cinema. I always tried to make California look like south London—or anywhere.

KAFKA: So a great film should be universal? Like *Greed*? Like *Living*? Like *L'Avventura*? Like *The Dark Knight*?

CHAPLIN: But we mustn't miss a great point. No country has ever known like America did how to make films for the entire world. Did you know, by the way, that for most of the twenties I was the best-known person on earth?

KAFKA: You were like a Beatle—and from me that's high praise.

HEMINGWAY: I hardly ever set a book in America.

WOOLF: *To Have and Have Not* is Florida.

HEMINGWAY: But I'd been to every place I used. I'd seen the mountains in the early morning. I'd tasted the wine.

KAFKA: And kissed the girls.

HEMINGWAY: Franz, listen to an old man, the girls in different places kiss in different ways—you're lying in a Venetian gondola with a girl from the city and her kiss is not the same as that of a woman in your sleeping bag in the Spanish mountains.

WOOLF: You must remember this—a kiss is just a kiss.

SONTAG: *Casablanca*!

WOOLF: And I doubt if anyone in the film had ever been there. The whole urge in movies is a fantasy. Film is for people who will never go to the real places. I daresay Welles made *Citizen Kane* because he wanted to dream of what it would feel like to be the most powerful man in America.

SONTAG: Ah! Now there you tempt me. He's most moving when he treats failed desires.

KAFKA: Mahler and Proust—they have the same theme.

SONTAG: The thing that rankles with me is that in a new medium, a

In the *Republic*, Glaucon argues that those who practise justice do so involuntarily… imagine something of this kind: having given both to the just and the unjust power to do what they will, let us watch and see whither desire will lead them; then we shall discover the just and unjust man to be proceeding along the same road, following their interest, which all natures deem to be their good, and are only diverted into the path of justice by the force of law.

twentieth-century invention, how is it that the best film is now sixty-eight years old? It seems indecent!

KAFKA: My dear Susie, have you considered: the movies were perhaps a spectacular rocket—rising fast and falling faster. Gravity's rainbow? You hear people talk of the golden year of 1939—*Gone with the Wind, The Wizard of Oz, Ninotchka, Mr. Smith Goes to Washington.*

HEMINGWAY: And Renoir's *La Règle du Jeu* was the same year—they come no braver, no funnier, no bleaker than that.

CHAPLIN: And *The Great Dictator* was 1940—nearly the same.

KAFKA: And *Kane* is '41. Perhaps the climax was there, with war as the perfect cultural setting for the movies. After that, was it downhill?

SONTAG: I don't want to believe that. I want to believe in the modern, the new.

HEMINGWAY: Daughter, in the war and in the years just after the war, more people went to the movies than have ever done since. And the population then was half what it is now.

CHAPLIN: Oh, you're right. You can't separate the movies from the crowd. It's a mass medium. Surely the greatest glories are the films that did the best.

SONTAG: *The Birth of a Nation?* It's a disgrace! Is *Titanic* the best film ever made?

KAFKA: Maybe not, but is Hans-Jürgen Syberberg's *Our Hitler* the best because so few went to see it?

CHAPLIN: May I say, in my humble way, that I was making short films during the Great War that kept people happy.

HEMINGWAY: The only people interested in keeping people happy during a war are the people who have organized it!

WOOLF: Oh, do we have to have so much dreary sermonizing? The films are like the circus. They are *silly*—really, I insist on it. They are meant to be silly. I referred to *Casablanca* earlier. Do you recall how by chance that film opened as the Allied troops entered the

Oscar Wilde's "The Decay of Lying," written as a Socratic dialogue, takes a different view:

CYRIL: Do you object to modernity of form, then?

VIVIAN: Yes. It is a huge price to pay for a very poor result. Pure modernity of form is always somewhat vulgarising. It cannot help being so. The public imagine that, because they are interested in their immediate surroundings, Art should be interested in them also, and should take them as her subject-matter. But the mere fact that they are interested in these things makes them unsuitable subjects for Art. The only beautiful things, as somebody once said, are the things that do not concern us. As long as a thing is useful or necessary to us, or affects us in any way, either for pain or for pleasure, or appeals strongly to our sympathies, or is a vital part of the environment in which we live, it is outside the proper sphere of art.

real Casablanca? It seemed providential. It seemed like newsreel. But look at the film—all that gorgeous romance. Who wouldn't love a Nazi like Major Strasser? And as for the idea that dear Paul Henreid had been in a concentration camp. He'd been in makeup all morning.

KAFKA: But people believed. And that Bogey fellow, he may have inspired real heroes.

CHAPLIN: After all, Mr. Hemingway, he was your hero, too, in *To Have and Have Not*.

HEMINGWAY: And then meeting that daft dream girl on a fantasy island!

SONTAG: But they really got married! Bogart and Bacall.

KAFKA: So maybe the greatest film is the one that makes the wildest jump from dream to real life?

CHAPLIN: Oh, Franz, don't you see, dear boy, they're the same. "When Gregor Samsa woke up one morning from unsettling dreams, he found himself changed…"

WOOLF: I like that idea—and don't forget that you could say, "Just before he died, Charles Foster Kane had a dream in which he imagined he was dying."

SONTAG: It does feel like that, like someone asking for just a few more seconds.

KAFKA: I wonder. We all say now, "I saw my life pass before my eyes." Do you think anyone said that before the movies?

SONTAG: It's true, the movies seem always to make us think about time and memory.

HEMINGWAY: You make it sound as if no one had thought about those things before. All narratives are physical models of time. Look at the book and the pages in order.

CHAPLIN: But the movie was for people who couldn't read! Can you consider the excitement we felt at the beginning when the movies came in? They had the power to move everybody in the world. The peasants and the professors!

Wilde makes a similar claim for great art:

CYRIL: What do you mean by saying that life, "poor, probable, uninteresting human life," will try to reproduce the marvels of art? I can quite understand your objection to art being treated as a mirror. You think it would reduce genius to the position of a cracked looking-glass. But you don't mean to say that you seriously believe that Life imitates Art, that Life in fact is the mirror, and Art the reality?

VIVIAN: Certainly I do. Paradox though it may seem—and paradoxes are always dangerous things—it is none the less true that Life imitates art far more than Art imitates life. We have all seen in our own day in England how a certain curious and fascinating type of beauty, invented and emphasised by two imaginative painters, has so influenced Life that whenever one goes to a private view or to an artistic salon one sees here the mystic eyes of Rossetti's dream, the long ivory throat, the strange square-cut jaw, the loosened shadowy hair that he so ardently loved, there the sweet maidenhood of *The Golden Stair*, the blossom-like mouth and weary loveliness of the *Laus Amoris*… A great artist invents a type, and Life tries to copy it, to reproduce it in a popular form, like an enterprising publisher.

WOOLF: *The Passion of Joan of Arc?*

KAFKA: Do you think that is silly?

WOOLF: The film—no. Though I always found the maid herself rather a pain in the neck.

SONTAG: And Bresson.

HEMINGWAY: Buñuel.

KAFKA: Fritz Lang.

CHAPLIN: Lubitsch.

KAFKA: Have you seen much Hitchcock? He is very interesting, I think. Sometimes, I wonder, just a little Kaf—

SONTAG: But he's no more than a common entertainer.

CHAPLIN: Oh, Susan, there is no such thing as a common entertainer. It is a noble calling!

SONTAG: Disney?

WOOLF: Gary Cooper?

KAFKA: Adam Sandler?

HEMINGWAY: That smartass Howard Hawks?

WOOLF: Ms. Sontag, tell me this: if you can't tolerate *Citizen Kane*—because it always wins—what would you prefer?

KAFKA: Yes. What were the runners-up in 2002?

SONTAG: I'll tell you. In descending order—*Vertigo, La Règle du Jeu, The Godfather* (parts I and II), *Tokyo Story, 2001, Battleship Potemkin, Sunrise, 8½,* and *Singin' in the Rain.*

WOOLF: Hurrah for *Singin' in the Rain*—such a lovely piece of nonsense.

HEMINGWAY: Every time the eggheads vote, *La Règle du Jeu* gets a medal.

CHAPLIN: And *Potemkin* still sails on.

SONTAG: *Vertigo* was second. A flop in its day. But taken more seriously every year.

In Plato's *Apologia*, offering a summation of his life on the eve of his execution, Socrates explains his own calling, and attempts to convince his listeners that they should treat it with more respect than they do:

And now, Athenians, I am not going to argue for my own sake, as you may think, but for yours, that you may not sin against the God by condemning me, who am his gift to you. For if you kill me you will not easily find a successor to me, who, if I may use such a ludicrous figure of speech, am a sort of gadfly, given to the state by God; and the state is a great and noble steed who is tardy in his motions owing to his very size, and requires to be stirred into life. I am that gadfly which God has attached to the state, and all day long and in all places am always fastening upon you, arousing and persuading and reproaching you. You will not easily find another like me... When I say that I am given to you by God, the proof of my mission is this:—if I had been like other men, I should not have neglected all my own concerns or patiently seen the neglect of them during all these years, and have been doing yours, coming to you individually like a father or elder brother, exhorting you to regard virtue; such conduct, I say, would be unlike human nature.

WOOLF: But it's so unpleasant. So cruel. And so preposterous.

KAFKA: Perhaps cruelty is man's last great faith.

HEMINGWAY: I like *The Godfather.* It's a very American story. A family story. And they eat good food and drink the simple Italian reds all the time. *The Godfather* won Oscars. It was a box-office champion. And I think it's damn good. It satisfies all requirements.

Total gross of *The Godfather* (part I): $133,698,921.

KAFKA: Fredo in the boat, saying a prayer. The shot sounding over the lake. This is very fine.

WOOLF: There aren't any women in it, for heaven's sake.

SONTAG: Have we all seen *Tokyo Story?*

CHAPLIN: No, I haven't seen it. Does it lift the heart?

HEMINGWAY: I think the heart is encouraged.

KAFKA [*Shyly*]: Do we have to decide? Must there be a winner?

SONTAG: No, I suppose not. But in thinking about the list, see how many pictures we are reminded of. The question provokes such an inventory.

WOOLF: It makes you want to see the films again.

KAFKA: Virginia, what would you like to see tonight? You and I, we can have a date.

WOOLF: *Broadway Melody of 1940*—I just adore "Begin the Beguine." It's pretty and smart for its own sake.

At this moment, a very large, weary, and perspiring man enters the café. He is laboring from the effort of carrying a large suitcase. It is Orson Welles.

WELLES [*Collapsing in a chair*]: For mercy's sake get me a cup of hot chocolate. And if you have any of those Viennese pastries—I'm absolutely famished for some reason.

WOOLF: Have you been on a journey?

WELLES: My dear Mrs. Woolf, I have been back to my past. Not a cheerful place, I assure you.

Women almost never appear as participants in the classical Socratic dialogues, either. The exception is a historical figure, Aspasia, one of the most famous women in Athens during Socrates's time. She is referenced in some of Plato's and Xenophon's Socratic dialogues, and was a major character in two other dialogues, one composed by Aeschines Socraticus and one composed by Antisthenes. Neither of these has survived in complete form, but in his *De Inventione*, a handbook for orators, Cicero relates a section of Aeschines's *Aspasia*, in which the titular figure takes on the Socratic role in a discussion with a man named Xenophon (not the writer) and his wife:

> Aspasia used to argue with Xenophon's wife, and with Xenophon himself. "Tell me, I beg of you, O you wife of Xenophon, if your neighbor has better gold than you have, whether you prefer her gold or your own?" "Hers," says she. "Suppose she has dresses and other ornaments suited to women, of more value than those which you have, should you prefer your own or hers?" "Hers, to be sure," answered she. "Come, then," says Aspasia, "suppose she has a better husband than you have, should you then prefer your own husband or hers?" On this the woman blushed.

Romantic attachments were always fair game in a Socratic debate. In Plato's *Symposium*, the jealous and lovestruck Alcibiades notes Socrates's prference for attractive young men:

> See you how fond he is of the fair? He is always with them and is always being smitten by them, and then again he knows nothing and is ignorant of all things—such is the appearance which he puts on.

Plato's *Republic* is wary of the idea that one's art can be all-consuming. Socrates asks, at one point, "And the interest of any art is the perfection of it—this and nothing else?" A conversation with Thrasymachus, who initially affirmed Socrates's question, ensues, exploring the peril of maintaining such a stringent commitment to craft.

Welles described this encounter in an interview:

> I had been called to read the narration for a film that [Hemingway] and Joris Ivens had made about the war in Spain; it was called *The Spanish Earth*. Arriving at the studio, I came upon Hemingway, who was in the process of drinking a bottle of whiskey; I had been handed a set of lines that were too long, dull, had nothing to do with his style, which is always so concise and so economical... I said to him, "Mr. Hemingway, it would be better if one saw the faces all alone, without commentary." This didn't please him at all... [He] said, "You effeminate boys of the theatre, what do you know about real war?"... and, right there, in front of the images of the Spanish Civil War, as they marched across the screen, we had a terrible scuffle.

CHAPLIN: Orson, we've been talking about your picture.

WELLES: Charlie, I didn't recognize you for a moment without a young lady on your arm. Which picture do you mean?

CHAPLIN: Why, *Kane*, of course!

WELLES: Oh, Lord, don't name that monster, not in my presence.

SONTAG: You don't like it?

WELLES: I cannot bear to see it, or to hear it mentioned.

CHAPLIN: Oh, Orson, come now! How can you turn on your own work—your own child?

WELLES: Charlie, I'll be candid with you, I have children—my own offspring—and I could not tell you where they are at this moment. My life has been work and magic, and I am the wreckage left behind.

HEMINGWAY: It is a hard thing to have young, but it is harder still to live without them.

WELLES: My dear Hemingway, that is very eloquent, but no comfort. Indeed, it reminds me of something less than kind you once said about me.

HEMINGWAY: What was that?

WELLES: I was recording the commentary for a film about Spain made during the Civil War, don't you know. And I was giving it my humble all, my very own Dublin Shakespearean uplift.

HEMINGWAY: Oh, God!

WELLES: Whereupon, you said it sounded as if I was swallowing my own come.

KAFKA: That's very good.

WOOLF: What did he say?

HEMINGWAY: I went too far. I have a tough edge.

WELLES: My dear sir, don't apologize now. You probably didn't go nearly far enough. I have a voice that hovers between sincerity and sham—I have since lent it to mashed potatoes, jug wine, and the history of mankind. It is a part of my charm, perhaps, but it is hard to live with.

SONTAG: It is a part of Charlie Kane's charm, too.

WELLES: Perhaps. I fear that Kane was given no option—it had to be me. Or be burdened with me.

SONTAG: Do you really not esteem the film?

WELLES: *Esteem*? I haven't heard that word since I knew John Houseman. Do I "esteem" the film? Well, I do not keep up with the garbage—I do not see every film made nowadays—but in candor I'm not sure that any one has surpassed *Kane*.

KAFKA: It *is* good.

WELLES: Is it? Who knows. It was once. It was as good as all the other Mercury people could make it. I never worked as hard on anything else. I never had as good a script. And I never had a studio as tender. Moreover, I was young—and I am one of those creatures who was born to be young. I managed it as long as I could, but then I yielded. After that I was a wreck.

WOOLF: So many of your thoughts begin with *I*.

WELLES: Take care, madam, or I'll send you out to Chicago to be my drama critic! You may be right, but you'll be cold!

CHAPLIN: Our problem is whether to vote for *Kane* as the best picture one more time.

WELLES: I know. The monotony of it. There's only one thing worse—trying to think of something that's better.

SONTAG: Don't you fear that with *Kane* voted number one decade after decade, young people will just stop seeing it? As if it was Shakespeare? They may become as bored with it as you seem to be.

WELLES: The boredom of ignorance is one thing. My own problem is knowing every frame and every cut. You see, as far as I'm concerned, the whole thing is one decision after another. And when a film is that cut-and-dried, I fall asleep. I need some precious uncertainty. But I lost that with every decision I made.

In Plato's *Protagoras*, Socrates is so put off by Protagoras's tendency to make long speeches that he nearly leaves. ("I have to be in another place," he says.) He stays only after Prodicus, another philosopher, pleads with both men to "argue with one another and not wrangle; for friends argue with friends out of goodwill, but only adversaries and enemies wrangle."

Much of Franz Kafka's most famous work was never finished. Many of the chapters in *The Trial* were left incomplete and have no clear linear relationship to each other. *Amerika* has considerable gaps in the narrative. *The Castle* ends in mid-sentence.

KAFKA: It's not settled, even on the shelf—that's Mr. Welles's point. I tell myself even now that one day I will rewrite it all. Make it really good!

SONTAG: So the more perfect a film, the more insufferable it becomes?

WELLES: Aha. Well, my friends, that is where I may be able to rescue you from your problem.

CHAPLIN: And how can you do that?

WELLES: I am just back from an exhausting trip.

HEMINGWAY: Where did you go?

WELLES: Rio. God, the memories that name brought back. I hadn't been there since 1942. Carnival time. [*To Woolf*] Have you ever been to Carnival?

WOOLF: I've been to the fair on Hampstead Heath.

WELLES: A very modest party next to Carnival. At any event: I went back to Rio, to the hotel where I'd stayed. It's still there.

SONTAG: Why did you go there?

WELLES: In '42, in Rio, I was preparing a film—a huge canvas—about Brazil and God only knows what. And back at RKO they were finishing the editing on *The Magnificent Ambersons*.

HEMINGWAY: Booth Tarkington. A classic Midwest novel.

WELLES: Exactly so, sir. Well, while I was there, they sent me a cut—my final cut. The picture as it was meant to be. And then— [*He shudders—the story is too sad to tell.*]

CHAPLIN: They did what studios do. They took it away from you. Cut it to shreds.

WELLES: They dumped forty minutes of the most heartbreaking stuff. You were meant to see the final decline of the Ambersons. There was a scene with Agnes Moorehead that would have established her as our greatest actress. It wasn't right for the war mood, they said. Well, it left the picture a disaster—my first great disaster, I suppose. And then years passed and I learned that the studio had taken the cut material and drowned it at the bottom of the ocean.

CHAPLIN: That James Cameron should do a film about searching for it.

HEMINGWAY: All our hopes begin and die in the sea.

WELLES: I daresay. The sea rolls on.

WOOLF: The waves, the waves.

WELLES: But then I remembered—there had been that print sent to the hotel in Rio. I never knew what became of it. Can you believe it?

KAFKA [*Breathless*]: Can we see it?

WELLES: It's all in the suitcase there.

HEMINGWAY: My first wife mislaid a suitcase full of my stories. It was never found. My best stuff.

KAFKA: I left orders for all my work to be burned.

SONTAG: I don't think I have the courage to open it. I'd rather imagine the film.

CHAPLIN: You are a romantic after all.

SONTAG: I always hoped the next book would be the real one.

WELLES: Just trust me, if you will—if you can. Don't you think the greatest film ever should be the one you'll see "next week"? *Coming attractions*, my dears—the warmest words in art or show business. Ladies and gentlemen, may I offer you the one film that could supplant that charming tyrant—Charlie Kane? The magnificence of *The Magnificent Ambersons*.

Plato's Socratic dialogues often ended in a state of confusion and doubt. In the so-called Aporetic dialogues, the goal of Socrates is not to answer a question, but rather to reveal that the preexisting answers are incorrect or deficient. In these dialogues, the final uncertainty is the whole point, as Socrates explains in Plato's *Meno* after conducting a thought experiment with one of Meno's slaves:

> Is he not better off in knowing his ignorance?... Do you suppose that he would ever have inquired into or learned what he fancied that he knew, though he was really ignorant of it, until he had fallen into perplexity under the idea that he did not know, and had desired to know?

GRAUSTARKIAN ROMANCE

LIFE SPAN: 1894–1927 AD

NATURAL HABITATS: Indiana, England

PRACTITIONERS: George Barr McCutcheon, Anthony Hope,
 Frances Hodgson Burnett

CHARACTERISTICS: Victorian utopianism, swashbuckling,
 courtly intrigue

The Graustarkian romance, which experienced a brief heyday in the first decades of the twentieth century, was a brand of adventure writing with one distinctive trademark: the stories were all centered on an invented Middle European country. At the time, the region was seen as exotic, but still close enough to the Anglo-American world to be recognizable (as opposed to the alien landscape of Russia and the Caucasus). The fictional countries—Ruritania was the first, but Graustark became the most popular—were located geographically somewhere near Austria, and chronologically in a world of Victorian nostalgia, of monarchies and roguish princes and damsels in distress. This world more or less disappeared after World War I, when the old kingdoms collapsed and sales of the genre dropped precipitously.

AN EXCERPT FROM

BEVERLY OF GRAUSTARK

a Graustarkian romance by GEORGE BARR McCUTCHEON

—1904 AD—

Beginning in 1901, George Barr McCutcheon wrote six novels set in Graustark, a tiny country he positioned between Romania, Russia, Austria, and Arabia. The Graustark novels made McCutcheon famous, but he disliked becoming typecast as an adventure writer—he preferred writing plays and novels set in his native Indiana. Beverly of Graustark *was the second in the series.*

FAR OFF IN THE mountain lands, somewhere to the east of the setting sun, lies the principality of Graustark, serene relic of rare old feudal days. The traveler reaches the little domain after an arduous, sometimes perilous journey from the great European capitals, whether they be north or south or west—never east. He crosses great rivers and wide plains; he winds through fertile valleys and over barren plateaus; he twists and turns and climbs among sombre gorges and rugged mountains; he touches the cold clouds in one day and the placid warmth of the valley in the next. One does not go to Graustark for a pleasure jaunt. It is too far from the rest of the world and the ways are often dangerous because of the strife among the tribes of the intervening mountains. If one hungers for excitement and peril he finds it in the journey from the north or the south into the land of the Graustarkians.

From Vienna and other places almost directly west the way is not so full of thrills, for the railroad skirts the darkest of the dangerlands.

Once in the heart of Graustark, however, the traveler is charmed into dreams of peace and happiness and—paradise. The peasants and the poets sing in one voice and accord, their psalm being of never-ending love. Down in the lowlands and up in the hills, the simple worker of the soil rejoices that he lives in Graustark; in the towns and villages the humble merchant and his thrifty customer unite to sing the song of peace and contentment; in the palaces of the noble the same patriotism warms its heart with thoughts of Graustark, the ancient. Prince and pauper strike hands for the love of the land, while outside the great, heartless world goes rumbling on without a thought of the rare little principality among the eastern mountains.

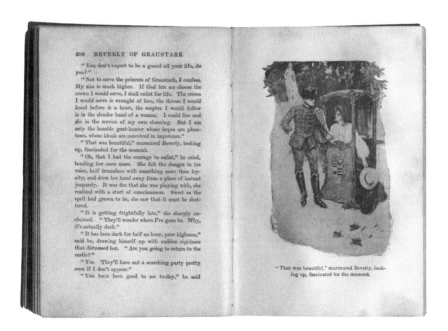

"That was beautiful," murmured Beverly, looking up, fascinated for the moment.

In point of area, Graustark is but a mite in the great galaxy of nations. Glancing over the map of the world, one is almost sure to miss the infinitesimal patch of green that marks its location. One could not be blamed if he regarded the spot as a typographical or topographical illusion. Yet the Graustarkians are a sturdy, courageous race. From the faraway century when they fought themselves clear of the Tartar yoke, to this very hour, they have been warriors of might and valor. The boundaries of their tiny domain were kept inviolate for hundreds of years, and but one victorious foe had come down to lay siege to Edelweiss, the capital. Axphain, a powerful principality in the north, had conquered Graustark in the latter part of the nineteenth century, but only after a bitter war in which starvation and famine proved far more destructive than the arms of the victors. The treaty of peace and the indemnity that fell to the lot of vanquished Graustark have been discoursed upon at length in at least one history.

Those who have followed that history must know, of course, that the reigning princess, Yetive, was married to a young American at the very tag-end of the nineteenth century. This admirable couple met in quite romantic fashion while the young sovereign was traveling incognito through the United States of America. The American, a splendid fellow named Lorry, was so persistent in the subsequent attack upon her heart, that all ancestral prejudices were swept away and she became his bride with the full consent of her entranced subjects. The manner in which he wooed and won this young and adorable ruler forms a very attractive chapter in romance, although unmentioned in history. This being the tale of another day, it is not timely to dwell upon the interesting events which led up to the marriage of the Princess Yetive to Grenfall Lorry. Suffice it to say that Lorry won his bride against all wishes and odds and at the same time won an endless love and esteem from the people of the little kingdom among the eastern hills.

It was after the second visit of the Lorrys to Edelweiss that a serious turn of affairs presented itself. Gabriel had succeeded in escaping from his dungeon. His friends in Dawsbergen stirred up a revolution and Dantan was driven from the throne at Serros. On the arrival of Gabriel at the capital, the army of Dawsbergen espoused the cause of the Prince it had spurned and, three days after his escape, he was on his throne, defying Yetive and offering a price for the head of the unfortunate Dantan, now a fugitive in the hills along the Graustark frontier.

Image from Beverly of Graustark.

FEASTS AND VILLAINS

a new Graustarkian romance by JOHN BRANDON

I

T HE ASSISTANT STARED at the suit coat in the closet. He wore a suit coat everywhere he went, and couldn't remember when he'd started this. It looked like a piece of someone else's clothing. The city outside the window was someone else's city. The buildings looked dopey.

He drew a hand towel out of the ice bucket, wrung it, and mopped his face. He returned to his reading. The sun would rise—in five minutes, in five hours. The Assistant had been scanning the same sentence over and over, a one-sentence paragraph that included a sturdy chair and a broad window and many other simple components of a simple room. The climax of the book was at hand, and the Assistant wanted to delay it.

He had been born in the wrong time. At least a century too late. He belonged in a place where it was difficult and meaningful to traverse one's country, where it meant something to die a certain way, where loyalty wasn't a weakness.

The Assistant was on an assignment. He wasn't a working stiff. He traveled. The work he did for Gary was unique and left him time to read. The work he did mattered. There was a window, a couple months Gary figured, during which the people would have it in them to rebel, and

Characters in Graustarkian romances are often restless adventurers, men unhappy with the modern world. In McCutcheon's *Truxton King: A Story of Graustark*,

> [Truxton] made up his mind to travel, to see the world, to be a part of the big round globe on which we, as ordinary individuals with no personality beyond the next block, are content to sit and encourage the single ambition to go to Europe at least once, so that we may not be left out of the general conversation… He was willing to go far afield in search of the things that seemed more or less worthwhile to a young gentleman who had suffered the ill-fortune to be born in the nineteenth century instead of the seventeenth… He was held enthralled by the possibilities that lay hidden in some far-off or even nearby corner of this hopelessly unromantic world of the twentieth century.

they were just now catching on to the fact that Gary needed rebelling against. They would wait for the boy and when he didn't show, they'd lose heart. And soon enough they'd have their savings accounts and their radio station and their history museum to keep them warm.

The Assistant was not to harm the boy. Gary had been emphatic about this. The idea was to dishearten the people, not to enrage them. If the boy was harmed, the people would know it. The Assistant's mark was Dunne. Without Dunne, the boy would never reach the island.

The Assistant could smell the burger he'd ordered from room service. He hadn't been able to smell it when they'd brought it, hadn't been able to eat it, but now its musty, broiled odor filled the room. It cowered behind its perfect little glass bottle of ketchup, glass bottle of mustard, glass bottle of mayonnaise. The Assistant rose and slid the tray outside. He dumped his ice bucket, made his bed, closed his blinds. He was hidden from the dumb lights of the city.

Gary had not been specific about how he wanted Dunne dealt with. He had made insinuations. He had made pointed insinuations, the Assistant had to admit, insinuations the Assistant didn't like the sound of. The Assistant went over and opened his door a crack and left it that way.

When the woman arrived, she did so with an even, conspiratorial knocking that pushed the door ajar a few inches. She came in and turned the deadbolt behind her. She began to take off her coat, but the Assistant stopped her.

"Looks like I got here just in time," she said. "You look about at the end of it."

The Assistant was standing now. He requested that the woman relax on the bed. He didn't like thinking about how close to the end of anything he might be. Maybe he was having a regular old hard time, like anyone might.

"Maybe you should have a seat here beside me," she said.

"I'm perfectly fine," the Assistant told her.

She shrugged, then went ahead and reclined on some pillows, let her feet, shoes still on them, dent the bedspread. She reached over to the nightstand and flipped the phone book closed. She looked at the Assistant expectantly, not rushing him.

"My name is the Assistant," he announced. "And I'm going to assist you in repeatedly climaxing, using only my right hand."

The woman didn't blink. "I'm the best in Missouri. Not the most

Practically every Graustarkian adventure focuses on the journeys of non-Graustarkians; room service is not usually included. In *Beverly of Graustark*, Beverly, an American, is initially confused when her Graustarkian escort tells her that they've arrived at "the Inn of the Hawk and Raven":

"I see no inn," she murmured apprehensively.

"Look aloft, your highness. That great black canopy is your roof; we are standing upon the floor, and the dark shadows just beyond the circle of light are the walls of the Hawk and Raven. This is the largest tavern in all Graustark. Its dimensions are as wide as the world itself."

"You mean that there is no inn at all?" the girl cried in dismay.

"Alas, I must confess it… I regret, your highness, that the conveniences are so few. We have no landlady except Mother Earth, no waiters, no porters, no maids, in the Inn of the Hawk and Raven. This being a men's hotel, the baths are on the river-front. I am having water brought to your apartments, however, but it is with deepest shame and sorrow that I confess we have no towels."

She laughed so heartily that his face brightened perceptibly, whilst the faces of his men turned in their direction as though by concert.

"It is a typical mountain resort, then," she said. "I think I can manage very well if you will fetch my bags to my room, sir."

The final book in McCutcheon's Graustark cycle, published nearly a quarter century later, was called *The Inn of the Hawk and Raven*.

expensive anymore, because I'm getting older, but the best. If you want me to come all over myself, that's what I'm going to do."

"Pretend I'm not here for a minute," said the Assistant.

"And I don't mean faking it. I mean I'm going to bite through my lip and the taste of the blood is going to startle me."

"Don't talk to me for a minute. Pretend you're alone."

II

Dunne had been in a sky lounge at the St. Louis airport for two hours when a sickly college-age kid wearing a puffy jacket appeared. Almost no one else was waiting in the lounge. The kid sat himself Indian-style on a chair directly across from Dunne and began clipping his fingernails. Dunne gazed at him uncharitably, but the kid's whole attention was focused downward on what he was doing. Underneath his jacket, he wore a tank top.

Dunne was antsy. His head itched. He'd felt unwell that morning, and had besides forgotten his deck of playing cards, and now was too stubborn to go to the newsstand and buy more. The cards were a custom for early arrival, a rule. Dunne felt he needed to suffer not having the cards so he wouldn't forget them again.

He checked his watch. The sun was peeking over the runways. He was going to someplace called Graystork. An island. Someone had contacted Dunne's employer at grave personal danger, he'd been told. The island's rightful leader, a woman of the ruling family, had disappeared. Her husband, a man named Gary, was attempting to take control. He was stockpiling currency. That was really all Dunne knew about it.

Dunne was carrying an envelope, which he hadn't opened. On the flap was written TO BE DELIVERED TO THE MINISTERS OF GRAYSTORK. That was his job, this time—to deliver the envelope. He also had a dossier, the kind his employer always liked to give him, papers full of incidental information. There was a map, an old-fashioned map on parchment, with dramatic illustrations. It was out of scale. Graystork was big as Texas. There was a rundown of Graystork's history and customs, also on parchment and written in a loopy script. The average Storkian, the pages professed, was quick to affection, fond of teamwork, fair-skinned.

More people trickled into the lounge: an old woman with a big beige hat incorporated into her hairdo, a group of men wearing identical sweatsuits. Dunne couldn't guess how many times he'd been in this lounge. They'd remodeled it twice. In five minutes, Susan, the attendant, would show up like clockwork and call him by name and give him a

In Frances Hodgson Burnett's *The Lost Prince*, the people of his fictional country, Samavia, are described as

of such great stature, physical beauty, and strength, that they had been like a race of noble giants... Among the shepherds and herdsmen there were poets who sang their own songs when they piped among their sheep upon the mountainsides... The simple courtesy of the poorest peasant was as stately as the manner of a noble.

little bow. Sometimes Dunne felt like he was in his prime, but more often he felt worn. He'd set up rules for his life and his job and had followed them, but these rules weren't aging well.

Maybe he needed to eat something. He didn't want anything sweet. He wanted chicken fingers. Dunne looked at the kid in the tank top, the frail nail-clipper. Eyes shut, he was swaying his head serenely. Dunne heard it now. Music was playing, drifty violin music that tried to blend itself in with the sounds of the airport. It wasn't a song, but a tamed swell of notes. Dunne wondered how long it had been playing.

Another bored traveler, on the road to adventure, in McCutcheon's *Graustark*:

Mr. Grenfall Lorry boarded the eastbound express at Denver with all the air of a martyr. He had traveled pretty much all over the world, and he was not without resources, but the prospect of a twenty-five-hundred-mile journey alone filled him with dismay. The country he knew; the scenery had long since lost its attractions for him; countless newsboys had failed to tempt him with the literature they thrust in his face, and as for his fellow-passengers—well, he preferred to be alone. And so it was that he gloomily motioned the porter to his boxes and mounted the steps with weariness.

As it happened, Mr. Grenfall Lorry did not have a dull moment after the train started...

Dunne always sat in coach. He believed it best to stay anonymous, and that meant avoiding anything first class. It was one of the rules he'd begun to wonder about.

The kid from the lounge was coming down the aisle. He stopped at Dunne's row and tossed something into the overhead bin, then slid into the aisle seat and labored to pull his seat belt out from underneath himself.

"Forgot my iPod," he said. "Can you believe it? It's a good thing they make their own music, where I'm going."

Dunne nodded as slightly as he could.

"My allergies are acting up, too. I'm not going to miss them, that's for sure."

The kid's voice was deep, but not like a man's. It was flinty, a boozy old broad's voice.

"I saw you fidgeting in the lounge," he said. "You're nervous about something."

Dunne gave the kid a look. The words *Mind your own business* came to him, but he didn't say them. His mind felt drifty, like it was out in the middle of the ocean in a flimsy skiff. Part of his mind was present; part was elsewhere, sun-stricken and starved. By the time the plane landed, he'd have a full-blown flu.

"I forgot my cards," Dunne said. "My playing cards."

"Playing cards? How quaint."

"I never forget them."

"You play solitaire?"

"It's my own game. A modified solitaire."

The kid fastened his seat belt. "Who are you?" he asked. "What are you called?"

"Dunne."

"Beverly."

"Oh," said Dunne. "I dated a girl named Beverly."

"Me too."

"Let me ask you something," Dunne said. He felt a twinge of freedom in his chest. He could exchange words with strangers just like anybody else. "You always clip your nails in public? Like where people eat?"

"I have special clippers. They catch the clippings inside and you empty them out later."

"But people don't know that."

"People don't know much," the kid said. He grinned.

They were taking off. Dunne watched the baggage handlers drive away, watched the runway begin to move underneath the plane. Some neighborhoods whipped past. When Dunne next looked over, Beverly was green. He was clutching the armrest.

"I'll be okay once we level off," he said. "I get this way in cars too."

"Do you take anything for it?"

"My stomach is bad. I mostly eat smoothies. I ought to have the one in my bag." He undid his seat belt, rummaged in the overhead compartment, and came down with a bottle of thick pink liquid.

"Take one of these out of the fridge, you have to eat it in like, two hours."

"Drink it," Dunne corrected.

"I get sick of them."

"They don't really put the weight on you, do they?"

Beverly shut his eyes. A serene look descended upon him, his eggshell shade returning. Dunne looked away. They'd reached the height where you couldn't tell, looking down on towns, what types of towns they were. They were all a scatter of roads, clusters of buildings strewn about like they'd been flung. Dunne was sweating under his clothes but he felt cold.

He lowered his tray table and took out the dossier again. Graystork was under Canadian protection, but was economically self-sufficient. It had been a commune since before the turn of the last century, and over the decades had evolved into a self-sustaining web of commerce. Everyone had a calling; hardly anything came on, hardly anything came off. Dunne suspected a joke was being played on him. Maybe the place was a theme park. Theme parks were big business, often dirty business. His papers said that Graystork had no real government, no elite, no concentrated wealth. The family whose job it had always been to oversee the place walked around like everybody else.

Dunne stuffed the papers back into his bag just as the plane hit

From book to book, Graustark, Ruritania, and Samavia were suspended between independence from and exposure to the political realities of their region. In McCutcheon's *East of the Setting Sun*, the country has nearly been lost in the postwar shuffle:

> "What's the name of that confounded little principality over in the Balkans? The one with the queer name."
> "Why my dear Judge, the Balkans—the rowdy old Balkans—were so mangled by the dogs of war that there isn't anything left of 'em to speak of... Jugo-Slavia swallowed a lot of those little states... I say!...You don't mean Graustark, do you?"

turbulence. A middle-aged woman staggered down the aisle and a baby cried out. The flight attendant announced that they'd run into an unexpected storm and were going to set down in Cincinnati. Beverly was awake now.

"Here's the storm," he said, as though he'd been expecting it. "Here we go."

"This wasn't in the forecast," Dunne said.

Beverly grinned again. "Forecasts aren't going to do us much good," he said.

III

Gary and the finance whiz finally met in person on a spacious catamaran moored to the end of a long dock.

"Some office," said the finance whiz, genuinely amused.

"This is where I have to take my meetings."

"Remodeling?"

"No, not remodeling."

"Unrest?" The finance whiz had a soft-looking spike haircut. He'd nimbly switched from amusement to concern. His hair was like leaning wheat.

Gary let out a slow breath. "Once you go on the island, on Graystork, you can never leave."

The finance whiz picked something off his thumb. "You told me that. I thought you meant I wouldn't *want* to leave."

"The natives can come and go. They don't, though. They don't go anywhere."

"I worked in the Middle East for a while," the finance whiz said. "They have plenty of rules you've got to keep track of. But this takes the cake, I think."

"It's not exactly a rule. It's complicated." Gary laughed. "My assistant has never been on the island. He's never been past this boat."

"Isn't this place Canadian?"

"Not really."

"So I'd live on a boat? That sounds interesting."

"No, I'd need you on the island. The compensation will be spectacularly fair, but the deal is you'll have to live on the island."

"You want me to start a bank here," stated the finance whiz, finding his way to familiar ground.

"A certain amount of resistance is to be expected. In what form, I can't

Bungled travel arrangements are a recurring feature of the genre. In McCutcheon's *Graustark*, a train is delayed in the Allegheny foothills, prompting Grenfall Lorry and the mysterious Sophia Guggenslocker to wander the town. Returning to the station, they find that the train has left without them, and are forced to risk a dangerous mountain pass in a stagecoach piloted by a drunk. Similarly, in Anthony Hope's *The Prisoner of Zenda*, Rudolf Rassendyll is forced to divert his itinerary from Strelsau to Zenda due to overwhelming crowds gathered in the capital for a rescheduled coronation ceremony.

Usually it's entering a Graustarkian nation that proves problematic, for reasons political and geographical. From *East of the Setting Sun*:

> It was no easy matter to get into Graustark. The little principality, beset on all sides by rapacious and more or less irresponsible neighbors, had been compelled to adopt strict and, on the whole, drastic regulations governing the admittance of aliens within her borders. Situated as she was in a great bowl surrounded by impassable barrier-mountains, she was in a position to enforce those regulations with the result that only those who came with proper credentials and could offer satisfactory reasons for their presence in the country were permitted to enter... Woe betide the adventurer who sought to enter by stealth or the smuggler who dreamed that craft would enable him to cross the border with his contraband wares...

say. Banks are, at this point, illegal."

"That's what makes it worth it to found one, right?"

"I think so, yes. You'd be in charge of everything. You'll start all the accounts from scratch and then move on—investments, loans. Advertising. Hiring. The way the branches would look."

The finance whiz squinted.

"You'll need time to think about it, of course," said Gary.

"Keep talking. I can keep up."

Gary went over and started a pot of coffee. He had a computer plugged in, a toaster. He handed the finance whiz a pale yellow brochure that listed facts about Graystork, projections, indications of its potential. He stayed quiet a minute, watching, until the finance whiz looked up, clearing his throat like an old man who'd been proven right.

"You'll get half the profits," Gary said. "Anything you want that's not on the island, I can get for you. I'm not a salesman. I'm somebody who doesn't mind paying for the best."

"I'd want some money up front. A signing bonus."

"That can be arranged."

"I've seen the world," the finance whiz said. "I've done all that."

"I'm not going to draw up a book-length contract. Whatever the bank makes, we split it. The women make good wives, if you're into that. Start a family out here."

"What does the currency look like, anyway?"

Gary pulled a bill from his back pocket and handed it over.

"Wow. It's canvas."

Gary didn't correct him. "I don't have cream out here. Is that okay?"

"Fine." The finance whiz handed the bill back and accepted a cup of coffee. He looked out the window. "What *happens* when you try to leave?"

"I honestly don't know," Gary said. "I haven't tried it. I haven't untied this boat."

That evening, back on the island, Gary sequestered himself in his room and played video games. When his dinner arrived, Gary shut the door and inquired about his wife. It felt outrageous to still have to worry about her, but she and her brother had him handcuffed.

"The gifts are piling up on the front steps," the houseman said. "People are waiting out there. They're wondering how she's doing."

"Do you think we have to tell them anything?"

In *The Prince of Graustark*, published in 1914, recent history has left Graustark's economy in turmoil:

The financial situation in the far-off principality was not all that could be desired. It is true that Graustark was in Russia's debt to the extent of some twenty million gavvos—about thirty million dollars, in other words—and that the day of reckoning was very near at hand… [but] the people had prospered and taxes were paid in full and without complaint. The reserve fund grew steadily and surely and there was every prospect that when the huge debt came due it would be paid in cash. But on the very crest of their prosperity came adversity. For two years the crops failed and a pestilence swept through the herds. The flood of gavvos that had been pouring into the treasury dwindled into a pitiful rivulet; the little that came in was applied, of necessity, to administration purposes and the maintenance of the army, and there was not so much as a penny left over for the so-called sinking fund… Private banking institutions in Europe refused to make loans under the rather exasperating circumstances, preferring to take no chances. Money was not cheap in these bitter days, neither in Europe nor America. Caution was the watchword. A vast European war was not improbable, despite the sincere efforts on the part of the various nations to keep out of the controversy.

The houseman sighed. "There's one of them trying to rouse suspicion. They ignore him, for now."

"Tell them she has a virus in her lungs. She's resting. Be positive."

"Very well."

"She's not going to commit suicide, is she?"

"Suicide?" The houseman was scandalized.

"Yes, suicide."

"I don't think she would kill herself."

This man was Gary's. Gary had hired him and brought him out here. He had offered him more money than anyone would ever need in exchange for his help in keeping Gary's wife locked in the basement. Still, maybe his wife was winning the man over. He brought Gary's meals and answered his questions, but the man's loyalty was elsewhere.

"She awaits the boy," the man said. "Her hope burns."

Gary sent him away. He began eating his duck. It was delicious, but he didn't have much appetite for it. He had to hope no one would decide that with his wife out of sight, his claim to authority didn't cut it. He had to hope her brother, the boy the whole island had such admiration for, didn't make it back. He had no idea whether his assistant understood how important it was to kill Dunne. That's what had his stomach upset: the thought of depending on his assistant. Gary had no allies here—not one. And he wasn't a good actor.

When the plane landed in Cincinnati Dunne went straight to the train station. He bought a ticket to Boston, where he'd be able to catch another train heading north. He went back outside and stood under the awning. He watched the rain make its way down in plump, unhurried drops. He had over an hour to wait.

Dunne let his eyes lose focus, aware of cars splashing back and forth, umbrellas bobbing past. He knew he should hunt down some cold medicine, but he didn't want to admit he was sick. He never got sick. He'd caught a bug and it would pass soon enough.

Someone was dragging a huge trunk toward him, shielding it from the rain with one arm. It was Beverly. "Jesus H.," said Dunne, knowing he had to help. He ran out into the rain and lifted the thing onto his shoulder, telling Beverly to get inside.

"I thought you were getting a flight," Dunne said, once they'd gotten back into the station.

"No. I believe I'll take the train."

In *Rupert of Hentzau* (Anthony Hope's sequel to his genre-inventing *The Prisoner of Zenda*), the Queen of Ruritania is similarly estranged from her king (although, to be fair, her true love is the king's lookalike, the protagonist of Hope's earlier Ruritania novel):

[The King] sought continually to exact from the queen proofs of love and care beyond what most husbands can boast of, or, in my humble judgment, make good their right to, always asking of her what in his heart he feared was not hers to give. Much she did in pity and in duty; but in some moments, being but human and herself a woman of high temper, she failed; then the slight rebuff or involuntary coldness was magnified by a sick man's fancy into great offence or studied insult, and nothing that she could do would atone for it. Thus they, who had never in truth come together, drifted yet further apart; he was alone in his sickness and suspicion, she in her sorrows and her memories.

"You know, they make suitcases that roll."

"This one's been in my family."

"Where you headed? You better get a ticket."

"Where are *you* headed?" Beverly asked.

"Boston."

"I'm going to go to Boston. That's my choice: Boston."

Dunne bit his lip.

"How about a travel buddy?" Beverly said.

Dunne felt like his will was under some rogue influence. He had already spoken more to this kid than he ever spoke to any stranger. The fact that Dunne had even helped him with his trunk was odd.

"I'm sorry," Dunne said. "I'm working."

"I'll be your sidekick."

He shook his head. His sideburn itched and he scratched it hard.

"I'm getting on the train to Boston either way," said Beverly.

"What I'm going to be doing, it's not that adventurous. It's not fun or anything."

"There's only so much adventure I can take."

"I'm going outside," Dunne said.

He went out and retook his position under the awning. Letting this kid buddy up with him would be against the rules, and sloppy—likely harmless, but that's what rules were for. You never knew which loose rock would start the avalanche, so you left all the rocks alone.

The raindrops were fewer and fatter. It was like each drop had its own target, and was being careful to hit it. Dunne glanced inside and something was happening, some commotion. He went in and a couple of people were helping Beverly up off the ground. A guy who looked like a PE coach clapped Beverly on the back, sending a tremor through him. Dunne came up and steadied Beverly by the shoulder.

"What the hell?" Dunne said.

"I fell asleep and slid out of my chair."

"You fell asleep?"

Beverly dug at his eyelid.

"You were talking to me three minutes ago."

"I get tired."

"Do you have that disease? You fall asleep walking down the street?"

"Not while I'm walking down the street," said Beverly.

Dunne went back outside. He breathed the heavy air. He patted his chest, feeling the dossier in his inside pocket. "Where's that fucking train?" he said.

In many of McCutcheon's books, a foreigner visits Graustark and is transformed by the experience into a hero, or even a prince. This tends to create a strange dislocation within modern men from England or America. Pendennis Yorke, the journalist hero of *East of the Setting Sun*, is not unaffected:

> He was thrilled—he was excited and eager. It was all so mysterious, so very puzzling, this extraordinary interest that was being taken in his welfare. Who was he that a whole trainload of people should be commanded to sit still while he crossed the trestle without fear of being jostled? Who was he that he should have a special kitchen, a special guard, special porters and a private automobile? Surely he could not be that inconsequential person he had always suspected of being Pendennis Yorke! No, indeed! He must be a person of considerable importance. And such being the case, he couldn't possibly be Pendennis Yorke. That explained everything. He wasn't himself.

IV

The train was two hours late. Once they left the station Dunne tried to focus on Graystork again. The dossier made him drowsy. The wondrous harmony was in peril. It all seemed out of a book, to Dunne. He rested his head, gave in to the rhythm of the train, and began to dream, aware of the dreaming as it happened. There was little visual element, only Dunne on a boat, going where he needed to go. There was someone with him; he couldn't tell who. Was this Dunne after his death? In his dream, Dunne heard a foghorn, gulls. He could breathe so easily.

When he walked into the train's lounge car, the first thing Dunne saw was Beverly, perched on a stool precariously, clipping his nails. The bartender didn't seem to mind. Beverly had changed clothes. He was wearing jeans and flannel. He had ordered a big daiquiri.

"A hero can never stay away from his sidekick for long," Beverly said.

Dunne ignored him kindly, taking a seat at the bar.

"Maybe you're not the one I'm looking for," the kid went on. "Maybe my hero's somewhere else, wondering where I am. You could be luring me off course. You could be acting reluctant so as not to spook me."

Dunne raised his arms off the bar and dropped them, giving up. He ordered chicken fingers and a rusty nail and it all came out in a flash.

"What's your first name?" Beverly asked.

"Major."

"I like that."

"I don't use it. People think it's a military rank."

"Mine's Clark."

"Your name's Clark and you go by Beverly?"

"Beverly's my middle name."

"Is that called steering into the skid?"

"Most places, I don't seem manly," Beverly conceded. "There's one place where I'm perfect."

"Where's that?"

Beverly didn't answer. He took a sip of his daiquiri through a straw. "Where are we going, anyway?" he asked. "What's our destination?"

Dunne took a tough pull of his rusty nail. "Graystork. An island called Graystork."

"Truly?" said Beverly. "I know a lot about that place. I wrote a paper on it."

Authorial self-awareness is not unusual in the Graustarkian romance. At the beginning of *The Prince of Graustark*, the fourth book in a series wherein American heroes and heroines continually marry into royal families, William Blithers tells his wife, "I don't take any stock in cheap novels in which American heroes go about marrying into royal families and all that sort of rot. It isn't done, Lou. If you want to marry into a royal family you've got to put up the coin."

"I'm worried about getting there."

Beverly removed the straw from his daiquiri. "You'll get there."

The Assistant was sweating through his suit coat, but each time he got himself up from his bunk and took the coat off he felt chilled. He'd finished his book and was experiencing the familiar loneliness of having read every word on a certain subject. The world had nothing more to give, at this time, concerning Robert Ford. The Assistant had fantasized, at one time, about writing a history himself, one sympathetic to Ford, a history that recognized that Jesse James's enduring fame was fueled, in large part, by the manner of his death, that recognized that it took more guts to kill a friend than it did to kill an enemy. But the idea seemed childish now.

The Assistant locked the door of his berth and sat on his bunk, grasping the gun. He'd done weeks of target practice. He could hit whatever he wanted to hit. He knew he should be walking the train, stalking Dunne, getting to know his mark, but handling the gun in private was all he could do just then. The gun was bluish. It was stodgy, but ready whenever the Assistant was. He dragged himself to a standing position and drank some water. He had committed himself to killing someone and he was no longer sure he could do it. Qualms, big and small, had schemed their way into the corners of his mind.

The Assistant had been Gary's right-hand man for almost ten years. Gary could get people to invest in anything, and the Assistant could work the kinks out of it afterward. Together they'd developed a system that rated works of art by a series of measurable emotional responses in the viewer. They'd developed a matchmaking protocol that put people together based on their tastes in movies. They'd developed golf courses in South Carolina. With this new project, though, this Graystork project, the Assistant had been little more than a henchman, or a secretary. He wasn't even allowed on the island. He felt nothing more than jealousy toward Gary at this point. He didn't admire him any longer. Gary was cunning and resourceful and never looked back, but he was like a teenager. He valued nothing.

The Assistant turned to the window, grateful to see the dry fields rushing past, grateful that time was indeed passing. He thought about the foolish woman on the island that Gary had tricked into a marriage. There was no such thing as divorce on Graystork. For a marriage to end, someone had to die. Maybe the Assistant was no less foolish.

Vladimir Nabokov's *Pale Fire*, with its references to the "distant northern land" of Zembla, both deconstructs and parodies the Graustarkian romance. Charles Kinbote, the putative commentator composing the material surrounding the poem at the novel's center, argues that his neighbor John Shade (the poet) was killed by an assassin named Gradus who mistook Shade for Zembla's exiled king. Kinbote envisions the killer and intended victim converging gradually, as the Assistant and Dunne do here. From *Pale Fire*:

We shall accompany Gradus in constant thought, as he makes his way from distant dim Zembla to green Appalachia, through the entire length of the poem, following the road of its rhythm, riding past in a rhyme, skidding around the corner of a run-on, breathing with the caesura, swinging down to the foot of the page from line to line as from branch to branch, hiding between two words... reappearing on the horizon of a new canto, steadily marching nearer in iambic motion, crossing streets, moving up with his valise on the escalator of the pentameter, stepping off, boarding a new train of thought, entering the hall of a hotel, putting out the bedlight, while Shade blots out a word, and falling asleep as the poet lays down his pen for the night.

He thought of Dunne. There had to be another way to prevent him from getting onto the island.

V

The train made it as far as Pittsburgh before it ran into delays that, passengers were told, would keep them at a standstill until sometime the next morning. Dunne did not have the patience to wait. He and Beverly set out for a rental-car office, Dunne lugging Beverly's trunk all the while. They made it to Avis just before midnight. Dunne chose a midsize and agreed to the insurance and when the rental agent, a tall woman with wet hair, ran his credit card, it was denied. She ran it again and again and it kept coming up bad.

"I could *buy* a car with that card," Dunne said.

The agent turned away to some paperwork, her hair sweeping her long back, giving Dunne a minute.

"Do they take cash?" Beverly asked.

Dunne shook his head.

"I have thirty bucks."

"Congratulations."

"Oh." Beverly unfolded his wallet. He turned flaps this way and that until he found what he was looking for.

"Try this," he said. "I got it a couple years ago on the quad."

Dunne cleared his throat and the agent came over and ran Beverly's card. "Eureka," she said, in a tone that chapped Dunne.

"I only got it for the free T-shirt," Beverly said. "And the girls at the booth were really tan."

Dunne and Beverly took the keys and found the car, and Dunne asked Beverly to drive a little while. He got him going on the correct road and set him up with toll money, and then Dunne delved back into his dossier and found that most of the remaining information was encyclopedia stuff—weather, agriculture, population. Edelweiss was the main village. There were no cars, just a few golf carts that people shared. There was a short account of how Graystork had become Canadian, dry political stuff. There was no crime. Crimes of all kinds were classified as "treachery," because any crime at all undermined the ideals of the island. The punishment for breaking the law was deportation, but no one had ever suffered this. Dunne looked at the map again. Graystork looked even bigger.

*   *   *

Edelweiss is the capital of Graustark in McCutcheon's novels. In *Graustark*, Sophia Guggenslocker describes her hometown to a foreigner:

> You should see Edelweiss, Mr. Lorry. It is of the mountain, the plain and the sky... Doctors do not send us on long journeys for our health. They tell us to move up or down the mountain. We have balmy spring, glorious summer, refreshing autumn and chilly winter, just as we like.

When Dunne awoke, they were at a gas station. Beverly had gone in, probably for one of his smoothies. Apparently the kid hadn't fallen asleep driving. Dunne was pleasantly surprised. They were ready to skirt Boston, and then Portland would loom up in no time. Dunne switched to the driver's seat. He thought about going in and grabbing cold medicine, but his cold had changed already. Now it was only a heavy head and a dry throat. As Dunne had predicted, it was running its course.

A knock came at the window and Dunne looked up at a weather-beaten guy with hollow eyes. Dunne took a breath, then pressed the button that rolled down the window.

"I have a proposition for you," the guy said.

"Yeah?" said Dunne. "Does it involve me giving you my change?"

The guy paused. "It involves me giving *you* money."

Dunne waited. He'd thought he was tired, but this guy looked like the walking dead.

"This coat is Armani," the guy said. "Quit looking at me like that."

Dunne waited still.

"I'm here because you're not needed on Graystork anymore. I got a pile of cash that says you're off this case. That's why I'm here."

"And you are?

"Who I am is the least important thing in the world."

Dunne peered toward the convenience store. He enjoyed when people attempted to bribe him. "I'm not getting out of this car. If you have something to say, I'd get specific about it."

"Specifically, I have a Chrysler 300 parked around the corner. First we drive to the nearest Bank of America and I give you eighty-five thousand dollars, then we put you on a train back home, wherever that is."

"Eighty-five isn't enough for a bribe. You need a shock-and-awe amount."

The guy's eye was twitching. "Eighty-five is what I can afford."

"Got to be like, two hundred."

The guy kneeled outside the car door. Now he was the one looking up. "I'm doing this on my own, as an individual."

"No shit," Dunne said.

"Don't get hung up on the money."

"What should I get hung up on?"

"I'm doing this because it's better for the both of us. I know things you don't. If you take my offer, you'll be doing the right thing for yourself."

Dunne looked toward the store again.

Anthony Hope's *Rupert of Hentzau* also follows the efforts of the ruling power's agents to disrupt the delivery of a letter. In Hope's novel, the narrator is a Ruritanian courier bringing a message from the sad Queen to her beloved in England. The constable of Zenda warns him not to let the message fall into the wrong hands:

> "Destroy the letter if there's any danger."
> I nodded my head.
> "And destroy yourself with it, if there's the only way," he went on with a surly smile.

"You have to trust me," the guy said. "I know you have no reason to, but what I'm doing is giving you a better option."

"I've never taken a bribe in my life."

"Well, aren't you something?" The guy suddenly looked like he might come through the window, and Dunne realized he ought to be wary of him.

"Get away from the car," Dunne said.

The guy didn't move. "You're going to force things to happen that don't need to happen."

"What things?"

"Bad things."

"I think we're through here," said Dunne.

"What do you care about this punk kid?" the guy said. "What do you care about that stupid island?"

"The kid? I care about delivering a letter. The kid's just a travel buddy and the island's just a destination."

"Just a travel buddy. That's what you think?"

The words were silly, Dunne knew: *travel buddy*. "Don't worry about what I think," he said.

"You're walking into something you don't want to walk into, okay? I don't know how else to say it. A hundred. Okay. If you're that stubborn, I can swing a hundred."

"Get the fuck away from me," Dunne said. "I gave you my answer."

The guy stood. "You're so sure, huh? You're a picture of certainty."

"I'm never sure," Dunne told him. "That's what's kept me alive."

"I'm not going to keep asking. Some people you just can't help."

"I'm one of them. There's no helping me."

The guy brought his hands together like he was going to pray. He turned distant all at once, like a gust of wind had altered him. He nodded slightly as if in agreement with his own thoughts, and just like that he ambled off, in no hurry, pulling his coat straight. Dunne watched him in the rearview until he was out of sight. He closed the car window against the gasoline fumes, trying to catch up with everything that had been said, trying not to think about the fact that a lot of it was probably true. Dunne didn't really know anything about the island or Beverly or the letter. He was used to being in the dark, but this wasn't a normal situation. For all he knew, that guy *was* trying to help him. There was a brick wall not very far in front of the car, and Dunne rested his eyes on it. It was smothered in so much competing graffiti it might as well have been brand new and blank.

In 1928, the *Literary Digest* reported that

Graustark and its capital city, Edelweiss, had been made so real by their creator that many a reader was convinced of their actual existence… eight tenths of [McCutcheon's] letters from strangers were written in the belief that these places had actual existence… [the readers] asserted or suggested relationships with the royal families of Graustark or the adjacent States, or with the American heroes and heroines.

When Beverly emerged from the store, Dunne got them back on the interstate. The rain had quit. There was a tint of light in the sky, tattered clouds strewn about the predawn.

Beverly sipped his smoothie and made a face at it. "When we get to Graystork, I'm going to eat a great feast."

"What, seafood?"

"Everything."

"What do you do, Beverly? You go to college?"

"I'm on break."

"What college?"

"State."

"Which state?"

"Does it matter?"

Dunne sped up to pass a U-Haul, then set his cruise control. "You had to write a report on Graystork?"

"They don't call them reports anymore. Papers."

"Right."

"I did a lot of research, looked at a lot of microfiche."

"Do you know what's going on there right now? Governmentally?"

"I'm aware," said Beverly.

"It's a pretty fucking important trip you're on."

"I know."

"The letter was expected yesterday, I'm sure."

"We'll get there right in time," Beverly said. "No need to worry."

"Little late in life for me to believe that."

Beverly touched his nose tenderly. "Who was that guy back there?" he asked. "That guy you were talking to."

"Junkie or something," Dunne said. "He needed directions."

"Where?"

"Couldn't really understand him."

"Which was he?"

"What?"

"Was he a junkie or was he asking directions?"

"Junkies never ask directions?"

"Rarely."

"I don't know what he was," Dunne said. "He wasn't making sense."

Graustark is always farther away than it seems to be, if not entirely unreachable, as the protagonist of *Graustark* observes:

> "It's a devil of a distance to that little red blot on the map," mused Lorry, pulling his nose reflectively. "What an outlandish place for a girl like her to live in," he continued. "And that sweet-faced old lady and noble Uncle Caspar! Ye gods! One would think barbarians existed there and not such people as the Guggenslockers, refined, cultivated, smart, rich. I'm more interested than ever in the place."

Outside Portland, Dunne pulled off to go to the bathroom. When he returned to the car and turned the key in the ignition, nothing happened.

He jerked the steering wheel back and forth, thinking it had locked. He nudged the shifter, making sure it wasn't in gear. He tried the key and tried the key. He sat, waiting to see if he was going to lose his temper. He let himself work through the moment. It didn't seem like he was getting too upset. Maybe the kid was right; you had to go with things.

Dunne woke Beverly up.

"So," Dunne told him. "Car trouble."

"I was wondering when that was going to happen."

"You can stop wondering."

In Burnett's *The Lost Prince*, it's the hero's hunchbacked sidekick (known only by his nickname, "The Rat") who appears revitalized as their journey goes on, despite all obstacles:

As the days passed, Marco saw that The Rat was gaining strength... he began to look less tired during and after his journey. There were even fewer wrinkles on his face, and his sharp eyes looked less fierce.

VI

Fog drifted into the cabin of the catamaran, in one window and right out the other. Gary was meeting with the woman who was going to set up Graystork's first lottery. It felt important to keep things moving. There would be a bank, and there would be a lottery, and Gary would control both and everything would be fine. The lotto lady had a flattering man's haircut. She wore a wool skirt. As Gary questioned her, he found himself becoming aroused. He'd long since quit trying to figure his desires. He offered her a tangerine from a cutesy wooden crate.

"There's only ninety thousand people," he said.

"You'd have to do a great job selling it," she said.

"We can't do the education bait-and-switch, like the States. The education system here is superb."

"You need a problem that requires money to fix." The lotto lady peeled her tangerine, dropping the fragrant patches of rind in her lap, a humble pile forming on the stiff surface of her skirt. "You need a disaster. Or a ghetto."

"I can do that," Gary said.

Dunne had always imagined the Maine coast misty and overcast, but sun was blaring in the windows of the bus, salting his eyes. Yesterday morning he'd been in a sky lounge and now he was on a Greyhound full of weirdos. Dunne was still wearing the same clothes. He probably stank, but he wasn't going to change. This was a one-day drop and he wasn't going to admit how late he was by changing into fresh clothes. Beverly had changed again. Before his trunk had been loaded into the bottom of the bus, he'd taken out a tracksuit and gone into the restroom and put it on.

Dunne choked down a banana. He didn't want to sleep. He wanted to count down the stops until they reached Sommenscot.

"I'm not letting you sleep," Dunne informed Beverly. "We're going to keep each other up so we don't miss the stop."

"Agreed."

"I feel very… not right."

Beverly nodded.

"You and I are going as far as Graystork. It's nothing personal. Whatever jollies you're trying to get, get them by then. When we get back to the bus station we're getting on separate buses. After Graystork, you're making yourself scarce."

Beverly raised a finger. "One thing. I think you were feeling not right before I came along."

"Know what? I changed my mind. You can go ahead and nod off."

"There's something you need to take into account," Beverly said. "Graystork, as I understand it, chooses people."

Dunne looked at Beverly. It was like staring into space.

"I read about it in my research. You're the right person to deliver this letter and that's why you're delivering it."

"I think you gave me your cold," Dunne said. "I thought it was going away but it's not. I never catch colds. I grew up with sixty other grubby-ass kids."

"I don't have a cold," Beverly said.

"This trip should be over. I should've been there by now."

"No one gets to Graystork easily. It's like this for everyone."

"And you've never been there before? Is that right?" Dunne could feel his scruff coming in. His eyes were dry to the point where it was difficult to blink.

"Never have."

"Then what's your business there?"

"None. I don't do business."

"Did you know that guy back at the gas station? You knew him, didn't you?"

"I've never seen that man in my life. I swear it."

"What a relief. You swear it."

"Get the map out," Beverly said, his tone tolerant.

"Why?"

"Just get it out."

Dunne unfolded his coat and pulled the dossier out. He spread the map and he and Beverly gazed at it. The island of Graystork now took

The concept of fate is central to the Graustarkian romance; often problems appear that can only be fixed by a particular individual.

At the beginning of *East of the Setting Sun*, Graustark has assumed this
kind of distant, mystical status. In
an early chapter, titled "What about
Graustark?", well-heeled men in
a New York City club ponder why
they haven't heard of the country for
a while:

The Publisher was gone ten minutes. On his return he found the
cronies in a state of drowsy reflection… It was easy to see that their
thoughts were of that far-off, tidy
little land in the turbulent East and
of the good old days when the very
name of Graustark stirred the imagination and played upon the fancy
of young and old alike—Graustark,
gray and strong and serene among
its everlasting hills.

In the 1960s, a horse named for
George Barr McCutcheon's fictional
country became a minor racing leg-
end. Billy Reed, a sportswriter, described the horse's final race:

As soon as the horses broke from
the gate, the mighty Graustark
began to draw powerfully away.
On the backstretch, it looked as if
the winning margin would easily
surpass the six lengths that then
was the stakes record. But then the
unthinkable happened. Suddenly
Graustark began to slow down…
in the last stride, Abe's Hope had a
nose in front.

Only later was it learned that
Graustark had run the last half-mile
or so on a broken foot. Imagine
that. Every time his foot hit the
slop, the pain had to be excruciat-
ing. Yet he still fought to the end,
straining to win. That was his
last race—but a young writer's
introduction to why generations of
Kentuckians have grown misty-eyed
at the sight of a great thoroughbred.
Even now, when asked to define
the elusive element that makes this
game special, a fellow's thoughts
turn to Graustark, laboring through
the mud at Keeneland on his
broken foot. This is class. This is
courage. This is racing.

up most of its surface, dwarfing North America.

"If you're not being straight with me," Dunne grumbled.

"I am," Beverly said. "We're doing great."

Dunne folded the map and looked past Beverly, into the bright woods. He could smell sea air, but could see no sign of the coast.

VII

The last land leg, between Sommenscot and the ferry, had to be traversed on horseback. At this point, Dunne expected no less. He and the stableman hoisted Beverly onto the gentlest animal and then secured his trunk in a harness on the horse's rump. Dunne took an old brown mare. He hadn't been on a horse since he was a kid. He'd forgotten how high up it felt. He and Beverly couldn't gallop or anything—the most they could handle was a horsey walk, a kind of shuffle. Beverly took his nail clippers out of his pocket. He held them for a time and then tossed them into the underbrush. He put on a steely look. The journey seemed to have aged him, or deepened him. He and Dunne clopped along without speaking, covering a mile. They'd missed the a.m. ferry, but they'd make the afternoon. It would be a two-day delivery—not so bad, really.

Abruptly, both horses halted. Beverly looked at Dunne and Dunne shrugged. They heard something, growing louder, an approaching gallop. A big, blond steed broke into view. On its back, holding on for his life, was the guy who'd tried to bribe Dunne. He still had his coat on. He was wearing cowboy boots with spurs. His hair was matted to his head.

"You again," said Dunne.

The guy was extricating himself from his stirrups.

"Yeah, you again," said Beverly. "The junkie with all the places to go."

They guy stood before them like a man prepared to orate, but Dunne wasn't in the mood.

"You followed us all the way from that gas station?" he asked.

"I was following you before that."

"Were you on the bus?"

"Yes, I was."

"Where?"

"In the way back," said the guy. "I had a magazine open."

Dunne looked at Beverly, seeing if he had anything to say, but Beverly was focused on his horse's mane. None of it had anything to do with him.

"Did you cancel my credit card?" Dunne asked the guy.

The guy nodded. He took a gulp of the spearmint air, acting as though he'd been summoned here.

"Let me guess," Dunne said. "You got two hundred thousand dollars together."

"No," said the guy. "I'm not here about money." He stood up straight. He was almost tall. "I'm here to fight a duel."

"Shit," said Beverly, impressed. He didn't look up.

The guy reached into a saddlebag and pulled out two pistols.

"You want to fight a duel with me?" Dunne said.

The guy looked Dunne in the eyes.

"What if I don't want to?" Dunne asked.

"Are you a coward?"

"I'm in a rush."

The guy bristled, as if absorbing an insult. "I'll shoot you. I'll shoot you right off that horse."

"Are those loaded? Don't wave them around."

"I traded a brand-new nine-millimeter for them." The guy removed his coat and draped it over his saddle. He fed his horse something from his cupped hand, having a moment with the horse, it seemed. The forest, suddenly, was quiet. The birds had stilled. "I will die, or I will live my life as the winner of a duel."

"You people are nuts," Beverly said. "You mainlanders are nuts."

"Some more than others, though," Dunne answered. "You have to admit, some more than others."

"Dismount, sir." The guy was away from his horse now, holding one of the pistols out toward Dunne, handle first.

"Are you sure? You're shivering. You're a mess."

"I'm sure."

Beverly opened a bottle of water and handed it to Dunne, and Dunne took a swallow.

"How long since you shot a gun?" Beverly asked.

"Maybe a year," said Dunne.

"Are you scared?"

Dunne looked at him. He didn't answer the question. He got down off his horse and accepted the pistol and stood in front of his adversary. The moment was rushing over Dunne. It seemed this was going to happen. He didn't want to give this guy confidence by stalling any longer. He didn't want to kill his own nerve by stalling any longer.

"Mr. Beverly will count off our steps," the guy said. "When he calls draw, we turn and fire."

In McCutcheon's novels, duels were often presented more as inconveniences, required to satisfy stubborn opponents, than as life-threatening matters. In *Truxton King*, the title character has the following exchange:

"Hobbs," [Truxton] said, "we've got to find John Tullis, that's all there is to it... I'm going to need him before long as my second."

"Your second, sir? Are you going to fight a duel?"

"I suppose so," he said lugubriously. "It's too much to expect him to meet me with bare fists. Oh, Hobbs, I wish we could arrange it for bare knucks!" He delivered a mighty swing at an invisible adversary. Hobbs's hat fell off with a backward jerk of surprise.

"Oh, my word!" he exclaimed admiringly, "wot a punch you've got!"

Dunne wrapped and rewrapped his fingers around the gun's handle.

"I want you to know my name," the guy said.

Dunne paid attention.

"My name is Riley."

"Riley," Dunne repeated.

The guy looked slowly from Dunne to Beverly to his horse to the colorless sky. He looked at himself. "You want to cock the hammer before we start pacing," he said.

Dunne did so. He cocked the hammer of his revolver.

"Do you have anything to say?"

"No."

"No prayer or anything?"

"Nope," Dunne said. "I'm good."

Riley nodded, being dignified, and turned his back to Dunne. "Mr. Beverly," he said. "Begin your count whenever Mr. Dunne is ready."

Beverly cleared his throat.

Dunne didn't share a look with Beverly. He didn't say anything more. He walked up behind the waiting Riley and shot him in the back of the head and Riley fell quickly and lightly. Dunne thought it had been quiet before, but it had not. The smoke from the discharge smelled of a task completed. Riley looked like a kid now, in a heap with his stupid boots on. No dust had been unsettled. No breeze blew. This was the first man Dunne had ever killed. The gun in his hand was heavy as a suitcase.

The first noise came from Dunne's horse, a firm guffaw. The horse knew in its blood that there was nothing to do but keep moving. The guffaw drew Dunne back into the moment from wherever he'd been, and he rested the gun on the earth, quietly, as if he didn't want to wake Riley.

A duel is preempted in *Graustark* as well:

"Is this a plan to prevent the duel?" demanded Lorry, turning upon the chief, who had dropped limply into a chair and was mopping his brow. When he could find his breath enough to answer, Dangloss did so, and he might as well have thrown a bombshell at their feet.

"There'll be no duel. Prince Lorenz is dead!"

"Dead!" gasped the others.

"Found dead in his bed, stabbed to the heart!"

VIII

The ferry was waiting when they reached the water. The captain was a crew of one, and he welcomed Dunne and Beverly aboard, heaving the trunk onto the deck, then went up and took the wheel and got them moving. The wind was cold in a welcome, bracing way. Rugged mountains were visible in the distance. Graystork was presumably straight ahead, hidden out in the fog.

"You can open the envelope," Beverly said.

Dunne disentangled his attention from the sea and leveled it at Beverly.

"What do you know about my envelope?"

"The job's over. Now you need to open the envelope."

"Let me enjoy this boat ride," Dunne said.

Beverly looked him in the face for what felt like a long time. Then he took out his wallet, flipped to a photograph, and held it out in front of Dunne. It was Dunne's employer, his arm around Beverly. There were more pictures, some a few years old, some from when Beverly was a child.

"He was a great friend of my grandfather." Beverly's demeanor was altered. His words were his own, but they had gravity to them. "You need to open it," he said.

Dunne was experiencing the sensation of falling. Some spray came and whipped his cheek. He felt tricked, and also incapable of being tricked. He felt confident in a way that had nothing to do with mastering his surroundings. He felt he'd made an agreement with the world, that he'd played the universe to a draw. He tugged the dossier out of his coat yet again, pushed past the map and the other pages. He found the envelope and handed Beverly the rest. He peeled the flap and ripped across with his finger. There were two sheets. Dunne took a look toward the boat's captain, whose full concentration was on the course he was cutting through the sea.

He is of the true line of Graystork. He is the only one who can preserve the island. Once on Graystork his every instinct will be correct. He will grow robust. The people will love and respect him. He will oust the interloper and he and his sister will govern.

Beverly was grave. "I wouldn't have made it here without you."

"Seems like it was your destiny. If it was your destiny, you would have made it."

"Destiny can be a fancy way to be ungrateful. People have a lot of destinies, and they need help achieving the right one."

"Feasts and villains, huh?" Dunne said.

Beverly looked down at himself. "Who'd have thunk?"

"Should I be bowing to you?"

Beverly raised a corner of his mouth. "I've been waiting my life out, do you know that? Everything I've ever done, I knew it didn't matter. Can you imagine living that way?"

Dunne didn't know if he could imagine it or not. Maybe he could imagine it better than he wanted to believe.

"Why didn't he just tell me you were the package?"

"You have to do it Graystork's way. If you're going to live there, it's best to come to a belief."

Disguises and secret identities are a common feature of the Graustarkian romance. Often, traveling nobility would assume false names for the sake of safety and discretion. While traveling in America, Princess Yetive adopts the name Sophia Guggenslocker (*Graustark*); finding himself lost in the country, Prince Otto maintains anonymity to stay the night at a farmer's house (*Prince Otto*); and in a more prolonged instance, Prince Ivor is raised as a poor vagabond named Marco, only to later discover his true identity (*The Lost Prince*).

Dunne's reaction to the letter's contents is relatively understated for the genre. When the villain in Anthony Hope's *Rupert of Hentzau* obtains the letter at the center of that book, the narrator describes the moment in this way:

> Another instant brought him to it. He snatched the pocketbook, and, motioning impatiently to the man to hold the lantern nearer, he began to examine the contents. I remember well the look of his face as the fierce white light threw it up against the darkness in its clear pallor and high-bred comeliness, with its curling lips and scornful eyes. He had the letter now, and a gleam of joy danced in his eyes as he tore it open. A hasty glance showed him what his prize was... the lips smiled and curled as he read the last words that the queen had written to her lover. He had indeed come on more than he thought.

"What do you mean?"

Beverly was quiet.

"What do you mean, live there?"

"We wouldn't have gotten this far if things weren't falling into place." Beverly widened his eyes toward the open water out in front of them, making a noise in his throat. "See it?"

Dunne peered. A dark form could be seen.

"Look at the other sheet," Beverly told him.

Dunne did, and what he saw was an official invitation to remain on Graystork. A job offer.

"It's permanent," Beverly said.

"No details on here."

"No details on Graystork."

"How much does it pay?"

"Enough."

"I'll live the rest of my life here and die here?"

This wasn't really a question, and Beverly didn't answer it.

"Why were you on the mainland?" Dunne asked him.

"That's where Graystork put me until it needed me."

The island was getting bigger on the horizon. Spires could be seen, piercing the mist.

"I wouldn't be leaving anything behind," Dunne said.

Beverly stepped over to his trunk. He opened it and took out a robe-like garment, then let the lid close and latch. He thrust his arms into the sleeves.

Dunne did not feel rushed or harried. He had no idea what he was going to do. A gull swooped, letting fly its peppy, shrill call.

The Graustarkian romance does not frown on a hero who looks out for his own advancement, as in this exchange from Hope's *The Prisoner of Zenda*:

"The difference between you and Robert," said my sister-in-law, who often (bless her!) speaks on a platform, and oftener still as if she were on one, "is that he recognizes the duties of his position, and you only see the opportunities of yours."

"To a man of spirit, my dear Rose," I answered, "opportunities are duties."

CONSUETUDINARY

LIFE SPAN: 970–1700 AD

NATURAL HABITAT: Europe

PRACTITIONERS: St. Osmund, St. Æthelwold, Luc d'Achery, Edmond Martène

CHARACTERISTICS: Prescriptive, proscriptive, fastidious, ritualistic

From the Middle Ages through the Reformation, monasteries throughout Europe kept detailed instructions for the day-to-day operations and customs of their respective priories. Written on parchment paper and unpublished outside of the monasteries themselves, these instructions were known as consuetudinaries. They informed each member of his specific duty, his daily allotment of food and drink, and generally served as a constitutional document intended to keep everything within the priory running smoothly. Read today, consuetudinaries provide invaluable insight into the longstanding traditions of a lifestyle closed off from the outside world.

A CONSUETUDINARY FOR THE REFECTORY OF THE HOUSE OF ST. SWITHUN IN WINCHESTER

—1349 AD—

The House of St. Swithun in Winchester's consuetudinary was recorded on two skins of parchment. It addresses a number of major and minor monastic concerns, specifying proper celebratory rites for feast days, explaining various important hygienic and culinary rituals, and noting the specific responsibilities of every individual member of the order.

II

OF CHEESE.

THE LORD PRIOR SHALL provide cheese, viz., a "Maynard" of 32 lb. every week, when he is administrator in the Refectory, daily from Easter to Quinquagesima before Ash Wednesday, and on Quinquagesima Sunday also, it is to be supplied at dinner and supper, but not on the three Vigils, viz., that of the Assumption of the B.V.M., that of All Saints Day, and that of Christmas; nor on the two of the four Ember weeks, i.e., that at Michaelmas and that in December before Christmas. In the Whitsun week cheese is to be supplied as on other days, and is not to be omitted because of the fast.

ITEM: on the Deposition of St. Swithun the Prior shall provide one cheese beside the "Maynard," large enough for the Convent and for the Monks.

ITEM: no cheese should be supplied in the Refectory unless it be good; and if any cheese be found bad let it be returned by the Refectorarian to the Prior's Storehouse to be changed.

III

OF BUTTER IN THE REFECTORY.

ITEM: the Prior shall provide butter in the Refectory twice a week, from SS. Philip and James' Day to the Exaltation of the Holy Cross, save on the Vigil of the Assumption of the B.V.M. On Rogation Days it should be supplied on Monday, Tuesday, Wednesday, and Saturday. In Whitsun week it should be supplied just as in other weeks.

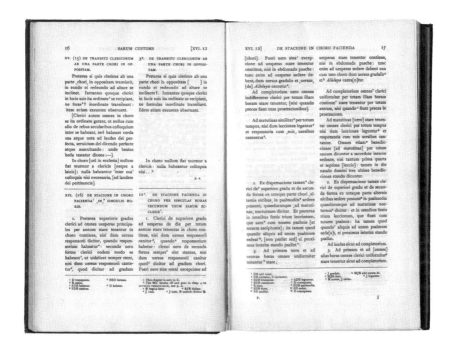

V

OF STRAW-LITTER IN THE REFECTORY.

ITEM: the said Prior shall provide straw-litter in the Refectory seven times a year, viz., thrice in winter and four times in summer. In winter, on the Vigils of All Saints Day, of Christmas, and of Easter; in summer, on the Vigils of Whit-Sunday and of St. John Baptist, and on the two Feasts of St. Swithun, that of his Burial and that of his Translation.

OF THE CHAMBERLAIN. OF THE REFECTORARIAN'S COWL, AND OF CLOTHS FOR THE TABLE.

The Chamberlain ought, according to usage, to provide each year on Palm Sunday one new cloth for the High Table, and canvas cloths for the other tables as often as may be necessary; and for each cloth he shall have a conventual loaf, for both the High Table and the other tables. He shall also find old cloths to cleanse the silver and the murrhine vessels. He is also bound to provide the Refectorarian with a cowl, according to ancient use, on Michaelmas-day.

OF THE PRECENTOR. OF HIS "PUNCHARD," AND OF HIS COMRADES WHO SIT WITH HIM ON DOUBLE FEASTS AT THE SECOND COLLATION.

The Precentor and his fellows, who, on Sundays and other days, at twelve o'clock after None say the Placebo, shall have a "punchard" full of good beer, viz., from Easter to the Exaltation of Holy Cross, unless hindered by feasts celebrated with copes or albs; and after the Exaltation of Holy Cross to All Saints' Day, on Sundays, unless any festivals should hinder.

ITEM: on every double feast the Precentor and his fellows, viz., they who do the great O, shall sit at the second Collation near the Refectory door, and shall have a pitcher of wine, and a "punchard" full of good beer.

ITEM: on all Saturdays it shall be done likewise, only they shall have no wine; and whatever is over shall remain in the Refectorarian's hands.

Translated by G. W. Kitchin. Image from The Use of Sarum, *edited by Walter Howard Frere.*

CONSUETUDINARY OF THE WORD CHURCH, OR THE CHURCH OF THE DEAD LETTER

a new consuetudinary by SHELLEY JACKSON

Issued by the Board of Dead Fellows of the Shelley Jackson Vocational School for Ghost Speakers and Hearing-Mouth Children (SJVSGSHMC)

INTRODUCTION.

THIS DOCUMENT, PENNED circa 1912 by an unidentified member of the Founder's inner circle, provides clear textual evidence of that turn within the Vocational School from a reverential but still essentially practical focus on the methodology of speaking with and for the dead, to a more devotional attitude. Scientific theory became tinged with mysticism; familiar sayings became codified into doctrine. Though still couched in the language of the schoolroom ("exercises" rather than "rites"; "lessons," not "sermons"), what had been pedagogical practices became elements of a weekly service that in its high seriousness had more in common with the Catholic Church's than with that of the Little Red Schoolhouse of yore.

This change can be tied to two events that deepened and complicated the Founder's understanding of her lifelong object of study: death. One was her maiden voyage to the realm of the dead (or, as she would name it, the Mouthlands), which she would describe as "a book with no pages but infinite stories" and "our forgotten homeland." The other and more

Consuetudinaries were not written by one single author—they were living documents of the monastery, occasionally updated to include new information. A single consuetudinary was intended to provide a flexible basis for living and worshipping over the course of several centuries.

Most consuetudinaries were not illustrated—but wax is an important and symbolic commodity in the genre. Different varieties of candles and tapers were used on specific occasions and in a particular manner, and several monks would often be charged with requisitioning them. Consuetudinaries specified precise weights and dimensions in each case.

It wasn't unusual for a consuetudinary to contain a prefatory note like this one, explaining the origins of the text and of the sect. *The Testament of John of Rila* begins:

This testament of our holy father John, citizen of the Rila wilderness, which he delivered to his disciples before he died, was rewritten from a parchment with great preciseness by the most honorable and reverend among priests, lord Dometian, a man of erudition and intelligence, who was a disciple of the reverend hermit Varlaam, who lived nine years on the Cherna mountain… [The testament] was rewritten for easier reading and for commemoration by all monks in that monastery, because the parchment on which the testament was written originally was hidden carefully together with the other objects of the monastery because of the great fear which was reigning in that time from the impious sons of Agar. In the year of the creation of the world 6893 and from the Nativity of Christ 1385, on the twelfth day of the month of February, on the memorial day of St. Meletios of Antioch.

conclusive event was the discovery on her damp pillow, after a restless night some months later, of a peculiar waxen object, which she recognized to be a word in an as-yet-untranslated language of the dead. The subsequent day,

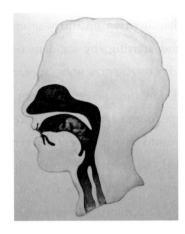

she closed herself in her study, allowing only her chamber pot and thrice-daily tray of graham crackers and milk to cross the threshold, and reemerged nine months later with mild anemia and a new cosmology. The land of the dead is made of language, she taught; we make a world whenever we speak. The dead inhabit it, and speak in turn, and die; the world they speak is ours. Gravity is a form of grammar. The planets obey the rules of rhetoric. "Death is the mouth from which we crawl, the ear to which we fly," she remarked, as she severed the blood-red ribbon draped across the tall, narrow doors of the Word Church.

Since that day, everyone associated with the Vocational School (faculty, students, employees, visiting aunts) has been obliged to gather on those hard wooden seats every Friday and indenture themselves to death—or, as the students say, "die." The Alphabetical Stutterers expertly halt speech-time, three hundred mouths backtalk furiously, and in every throat the dead rise up. The chapel fills with the ambiguous air of the Mouthlands, in which fleeting notions have the presence of two-thousand-year-old megaliths, and material things look at you like distant cousins, and nothing you have ever done is what you thought it was. The Thanatomaths pitch themselves through their own mouths, showing the whole congregation their "red" or "tonsil" faces, and strike out into death. Outside, the cries of birds rise up like a wall of thorns.

In theory, the Word Church needs no consuetudinary, since in it, every day is the same day—namely, the first day the Founder led the congregation in hailing the dead. Its time-reversal techniques are meant to transport every mouth back to the previous service, when another mouth stood open in its place, so that it can transmit what that mouth said without alteration. That mouth which was itself channeling a previous speaker, who was channeling another, who was channeling another, and so on, all these mouths tunneling backward through history forming a sort of ear trumpet through which resonates the very first of the series: the voice of the dead Clive Matty, speaking through the Founder at that reverberant first service.

In practice, of course, minor differences in the embouchure of speakers—a lisp here, an overbite there—add up. The ear trumpet gets a kink in it, and then another, until nothing can be heard at all. In such cases, the following procedures will recalibrate the faulty instrument.

The original of this text, laboriously handwritten on thirty-seven pages of an otherwise empty notebook and starting, by accident or design, at its intended end (thus the words COMPOSITION BOOK appear on the back cover, upside down), was until now the sole existing copy, since the SJVS chose never to set it into type, out of simple negligence or a superstitious conviction that to do so would only remove it further from its source. Some effort was expended, however, on making it *appear* machine-printed: the letters are minute and bristle with serifs like little hooks (inducing a half-conscious discomfort in the throat-clearing reader). The pretense is carried so far as the travesty of an "engraving"—really, pen and ink—on the title page, depicting an open mouth, very clumsily rendered, with more teeth than is typical in *Homo sapiens sapiens*.

CONSUETUDINARY OF THE WORD CHURCH.

I. *Of the structure of the Church, disposition of its Congregation, etc.*

II. *Of the several Bodies of the Congregation.*

III. *Of the manner in which the Vocation is to be practiced day and night throughout the year.*

IV. *Of the manner in which the Friday office shall fittingly be carried out; with the rituals, their order, and their occasions.*

V. *Of the Liturgies.*

VI. *Of the Readings.*

VII. *Of the use of Sacramental Ink, Saliva, and Chewed Paper.*

VIII. *Of the use of Gags, Prosthetic Mouths, etc.*

IX. *Of Signs that may be used during the Offices.*

X. *Of the Services that the Pupils shall render to the Community.*

XI. *Of the Manner in which a dead Pupil shall be sent into the Mouthlands.*

In his introduction to *A Consuetudinary of the Fourteenth Century for the Refectory of the House of St. Swithun in Winchester*, G. W. Kitchin writes,

> The document, which is written on two skins of fine white parchment, and is 3 feet 4 inches long and 11 inches broad, is by no means easy to read. For it not only belongs to a time when the general handwriting was becoming much contracted, but it has also suffered much from careless usage. It probably lay about in the Refectory, was taken up and thumbed by the Monks, curious to learn their own, and, still more, their neighbours' duties, until in some parts the parchment has grown brown, and the writing is here and there almost obliterated; nor has the difficulty of reading it been diminished by the carelessness of some good Brother, who spilt his beer on the back of it.

A partial table of contents from the House of St. Swithun in Winchester consuetudinary:

I

OF THE STRUCTURE OF THE CHURCH, DISPOSITION OF ITS CONGREGATION, ETC.

Since consuetudinaries were written for specific churches and cathedrals, the physical structure of the place of worship was often quite important to the particulars of each ritual. *The Use of Sarum*, a consuetudinary written by St. Osmond (patron saint of insanity) during his time as Bishop of Salisbury, was intended for the cathedral being built at Old Sarum, of which R. B. Pugh and Elizabeth Crittall write,

> It lay in the northwest quarter of the Saxon town, later known as Old Salisbury, within the new Norman castle on the peak of the high mound. The general plan of the church reflected the most common Norman practice of three apses (i.e., an apsidal east end, and north and south transepts with eastern apses) and solid walls for the choir…
> It was not ready for consecration until 1092, and five days later was struck by lightning and partially destroyed.

Clothing was heavily regulated in a consuetudinary. In his preface to a reprinting of the *Customary of the Benedictine Monasteries of Saint Augustine, Canterbury, and Saint Peter, Westminster*, Edward Maunde Thompson observes, "Regulations against gaiety in dress are naturally strict. We notice that gloves with fingers, 'distinctae per digitos,' are among the vanities, 'inordinata,' which are to be eschewed."

The campus of the Vocational School is to its chapel as throat and lungs are to the mouth and ear. Thus, contrary to casual usage, the Word Church correctly conceived is not only the building specifically set aside for devotions, but the entire complex, while the rituals of the classroom, refectory, and sleeping quarters are as sacramental as those of the service.

The Vocational School is a huddle of elderly buildings (formerly the Cheesehill Home for Wayward Girls, among them the Founder's own mother), much abused by the weather and dank even in summer. The chapel is a newer building, raised under the direction of the Founder herself like a shushing finger held up to the sky, but it does not look out of keeping beside the Cheesehill structures. Tiered like an operating theater—or like an ear with its whorls—it also possesses a ridged ceiling something like the ribbed vault of a Gothic cathedral, but more like the roof of a mouth.

The congregate Tongue in the chapel's center comprises the Hearing-Mouth Children in Training, in red flannel short pants and jackets and caps. Sharp corrective Teeth line the first tier above it, dressed in peaked cowls of starched flannel of an ivory hue. The middle tiers, called *Rebuke*, *Reproach*, and *I'm disappointed in you*, are occupied by the rest of the congregation—kitchen staff, maids, groundskeepers, and those of the general public admitted by the Dead Fellows through their mouthpiece, the Doorkeeper. Advanced Ghost Speakers, or Salivary, dressed in peaked cowls of starched flannel of a cardinal hue, with about their necks a large, pink, molded papier-mâché collar something like the Egyptian *usekh*, called an Uvula (but actually representing the entire pharyngeal opening), move freely among those in this section, some bearing such devotional objects as spittoons, gags, etc., others with the white balloons that represent the Dead Fellows (or, say believers, contain them). The highest tiers are reserved for the use of the dead.

At the focus of the theater is the chancel, where the choir is ranged in ascending tiers, those on the left being stutterers, and those on the right being stammerers. The two parts of the choir flank a very great Hole, angled downward and terminating out of sight of the congregation, with at the bottom a stoup to be kept brimming with the saliva of the devout, which is collected in spittoons at intervals throughout the ceremony, and borne down with all due pomp. In front of the Hole, though not completely blocking it from view, is a black screen with a small perforation in it through which the mouth of the Headmistress, by custom heavily rouged, may address the congregation.

Recesses to either side house the Wrong Tree (to the left of the hole; shown at right) and a small library for mastication (to the hole's right). On unoccupied stretches of wall, where in a Christian church one might expect to find sacred art, chalk-boards serve as a reminder of the classroom origins of the service, as well as permitting speakers to illustrate their points with impromptu diagrams.

II

OF THE SEVERAL BODIES
OF THE CONGREGATION.

The *Headmistress*, or Mistress Jackson.

The *Board of Dead Fellows*, represented by balloons.

The Advanced Ghost Speakers, or *Salivary*.

The *Teeth*, advanced students charged with the task of discipline.

The Hearing-Mouth Children in Training,
collectively composing the *Tongue*.

The *Choir* or *Alphabet in Absentia*, which has two parts: the *Stutterers*—
those who balk at consonants; and the *Stammerers*—
those who balk at vowels.

The general congregation, or *Vocabulary*.

The dead.

III

OF THE MANNER IN WHICH THE VOCATION
IS TO BE PRACTICED DAY AND NIGHT
THROUGHOUT THE YEAR.

The school is the church, the church is the school; thus all the Hearing-Mouth Children's studies are to be considered devotions. All speech communes with the dead, and everything that happens in the mouth is speech, and is performed with due solemnity. Eating is inward speech

Some of the offices of the Refectory of the House of St. Swithun:

The Prior
The Chamberlain
The Refectorarian
The Sacrist
The Precentor
The Almoner
The Cook
The Gardener
The Guardian of the Altar of
    the Virgin Mary
The Cellarar
The Curtarius
The Refectorarian's Valet
The Porter

and should be pronounced carefully; hiccups should be heard, not cured, etc.

The order of the day (on all days except Friday, when all must repair to the chapel for devotions) for children in the early stages of training is:

Consuetudinaries often provided incredibly detailed instructions for the daily life of the monastics, particularly for the youngest members of the order. In *The English Black Monks of St. Benedict*, Ethelred Luke Taunton explains,

> During their year's probation the novices never eat meat except under most extraordinary circumstances. There are minute directions about changing their clothes and the times, places, and manner thereof; about the care of the lavatory and personal cleanliness; about blood-letting and the bath, &c.

And Edward Maunde Thompson, in his *Customary of the Benedictine Monasteries* preface, writes:

> The extraordinary minuteness of detail in regulations and instructions framed to meet all possible contingencies was the natural outcome of life passed in a confined society, in which one day literally telleth another, shut off from the distractions and, we may add, the alleviations of the outer world, and forming indeed a little world of its own; and it was necessary in a society whose discipline had to be controlled by many heads of departments, to use a modern phrase, whose particular spheres of action had to be strictly defined and each one fenced about against possible encroachments from its neighbours. To one who has passed a life in the bonds of official routine there is a certain air in many of the regulations of these Benedictine monasteries which irresistibly, nay, even whimsically, recalls others not very far removed from his own time. Thus, when we read that the dormitory bell was to be supplied by the sacrist, but that the chamberlain was to find the bell-rope and to keep it in repair, we only recognize with a smile an instance of that division of responsibility which is so well appreciated in more than one of our public departments.

5:00 a.m.: Mouth inspection, scrapings, tonsil smears, collection of sponges, crutches, and training devices. Any mouth objects to be reported to the *Teeth*.

5:30 a.m.: Ablutions, with special attention to the purity of the tongue.

6:00 a.m.: Throat clearing, oral calisthenics, and lip stretches. For the older children, strength training. On Tuesdays, the tongue to be struck with wires.

7:00 a.m.: Concrete Inward Speech I, or "breakfast."

8:00 a.m.: Silence and voice training (stuttering practice, tongue twisters, silence scales, and arpeggios).

9:00 a.m.: Word games (as, What Is in the Box, Coffeepot, etc).

10:00 a.m.: Thanatology and thanatography.

12:00 p.m.: Concrete Inward Speech II ("lunch").

1:00 p.m.: Self-Erasure, Playing Dead, etc.

2:00 p.m.: Invocations.

3:00 p.m.: Recess.

4:00 p.m.: For the younger children, silent study or special activities; for advanced students, Ghost Speaking, translations, etc.

6:00 p.m.: Address by the Headmistress.

6:30 p.m.: Concrete Inward Speech III ("dinner").

7:30 p.m.: Readings from the Founder's devotional texts, the Analects. On Monday, the text shall be that beginning, "Good morning, Mr. Hoptoad." Tuesday, "We were walking on a country road bestrewn with obstacles, obstacles that arose from language itself and spoke rudely to us," etc. Wednesday, "— got your tongue?" Thursday, "Yes, it isn't," etc. Friday, "By blowing through the windpipe of an animal soon after it is slain, you can produce a sound very similar to the natural voice of the animal." Saturday,

"*Ta-ma-ha-ma-ka*!" Sunday, "I could not open my mouth, but I opened the world in which my mouth was," etc.

8:00 p.m.: Ablutions and kitting up, i.e., installation of sponges and/or individual training devices as crutches, braces, tongue rugs, personal mouth theaters.

8:30 p.m.: Mouth inspection and lubrication.

9:00 p.m.: Bed.

IV

OF THE MANNER IN WHICH THE FRIDAY OFFICE SHALL FITTINGLY BE CARRIED OUT; WITH THE RITUALS, THEIR ORDER, AND THEIR OCCASIONS.

So that each member of the congregation may pass through all the stations of the mouth journey, each of the eighteen parts of the following service symbolically recapitulates one important stage in the Founder's life.

i—She *was born*, with obvious reluctance, like something said very slowly but with great force.

> THE EXERCISE: The entire congregation stands with mouths ajar as a lone Stammerer (I-concentration) sings, "I am the hole through which I will pour myself into nothingness and this torrent is precisely my life," etc. The Salivary may weep, beat their breasts, tear x, etc., as moved to do so by what may be understood as a kind of funeral for one departing nonexistence and being, as it were, buried in life (in a pink, stinking animal coffin).
>
> As the remainder of the exercise is performed by the dead, who require no instruction, it need not be detailed here.

ii—She *breathed*, a simple form of speech.

> THE EXERCISE: A small mammal, freshly killed, is played upon as a bagpipe, holes being punched in the windpipe for this purpose, and fitted with straws to permit controlled egress of breath.

iii—She *cried*, perhaps realizing that many years would pass before she would rejoin the infinite Vocabulary. "In my howls I found some

Music was essential to the monastery, and consuetudinaries often included notation for hymns used in the course of ceremonies. The below appears in *The Use of Sarum*:

comfort and thus learned my first lesson about language: that one might host what one could neither master nor become, for in a sob weep all the generations past and to come; a wail is all words, all languages at once." The newborn's mouth opens directly onto the Mouthlands, and through it all our ancestors shout at us— instructions, pleas, queries. (*Have you forgotten me? Did you ever find the recipe I lost behind the fridge?*)

THE EXERCISE: Synchronized sobbing, with hand gestures. Amateur weepers are led through the complex variations of this exercise by a series of simple analogies (cry like a gun, now like a drain, etc.). *Teeth* to circulate with sponges lashed to the ends of sticks, dabbing up tears to be decanted into an Erlenmeyer flask, corked, labeled with the date, and archived in the library under "Wet Speech."

iv—She *sucked*, and later *ate*: a form of listening.

THE EXERCISE: A small coffin (made of potato flour and water, and distributed at the door) to be lowered into every mouth. Accompanied by the gnashing of Teeth.

v—She *pissed* and *shat*, forms of concrete speech.

THE EXERCISE: Approved knots for the face diaper are more easily diagrammed than explained; see below. Some satellite schools and home study groups now use commercially available disposables such as the TalkWad™, with their convenient elasticized speech pouches, but the SJVS proper has always insisted on the old cloth diaper, its ineradicable stains telling a rich story of oral hygiene through regulated speech.

Eating was more often treated as an obstruction to listening. In *The English Black Monks of St. Benedict*, Taunton writes of mealtimes:

No noise to be made; for instance, if there are nuts, they are not to be cracked with the teeth, but a monk is privately to open them with his knife, so as not to disturb the reader. Should he spill anything, he has to go and do penance in the middle of the refectory if strangers are not present. He is not to make signs across the refectory, not to look about or watch what the others are doing; he is not to lean on the table; his tongue and eyes are to be kept in check, and the greatest modesty observed. His ears, however, are always to be attentive to the reading and his heart fixed on his heavenly home.

vi—She *puked*, another early form of writing.

> After a picnic of cold borscht and hot kielbasa, she was obliged to utter something guttural in the water closet, and emerged afterward with a preoccupied look. In conjunction with a bout of spastic colon occurring some months later, this incident gave rise to a fruitful confusion between the "right" and "wrong" end of a person and what was supposed to come out of it. "I have something to say," would precede a visit to the water closet, from which might issue the sounds of a protracted argument. The insight that language might be concrete (and even as a wind carried a whiff of matter) was a valuable one, whatever its derivation.

> > THE EXERCISE: Salivary to remove the Uvula, lifting it over their heads, invert it to show its dark underside, and hold it out toward each member of the congregation in turn. The latter ceremoniously inclines his head through the opening in a gesture that economically refers both to the passage of food through the esophagus and the characteristically suppliant pose of those confiding something private to their commode.

vii—She *babbled*. The Founder often spoke of this period as a Golden Age, in which the universal Voice had not yet been trussed up in words all too easily mistaken for her own. Her attempt to assemble an Organ of Babies to serve as privy council, drawn from Cheesehill and environs, was thwarted by prejudice and restraining orders, the latter obtained by several mothers from no doubt well-compensated functionaries of the law after the Founder's delightfully enthusiastic but perhaps ill-advised and certainly horribly misunderstood Springtime Snatch. (Anyone lucky enough to have been there will remember the glorious cacophony of infant voices raised in concert, while the Founder dashed back and forth, encouraging the quiet ones with blows from a small mallet, like a xylophone player at a giant instrument.)

> > THE EXERCISE: Tongue twisters, including those in foreign languages, to be rapidly recited by entire congregation, then by the choir alone. "Mistakes" to be noted and added to the liturgy of mispronounced words.

In the less remote monasteries of England, local villages and even individuals found their way into consuetudinaries as sponsors of the monks' work. *A Consuetudinary of the Fourteenth Century for the Refectory of the House of St. Swithun in Winchester* instructs:

> The Refectorarian shall provide seven Branches to burn at the foot of the Cross, for a certain revenue of eighteen-pence... to be obtained from a certain rent in Parchemer-street, by gift of Geoffry le Barbour, on the south side, almost at the end of that street towards the City walls: and yet Geoffry's Charter does not mention that street, but the street called Fleshmonger-street; so that it is not known whether the tenement of the said Geoffry was in the one street or in the other.

viii—She *listened*. To her rabbits, primarily, mainly before they were slaughtered and strung up for sale in her family's roadside stand.

This early and oft-repeated encounter with the loss of a loved one deepened the thanatological insights of the budding genius, who even in her last years still spent many hours in consultation with her rabbits, listening closely to words no others could hear.

THE EXERCISE: Hoop-shaped ear trumpets are distributed. Beginners will place one end in the ear, the other in the mouth, and hold a private colloquy; more advanced students will reverse the trumpet, allowing the Hearing Mouth to enjoy the confidences of the Speaking Ear.

In some monasteries, speech was much less celebrated. *The English Black Monks of St. Benedict* explains:

> The monk's life was largely spent in the cloister. There all sat in order and in fixed places. No one was allowed to go outside the cloister without leave. Silence was always observed save on certain days and times when conversation was allowed. At other times, they had to obtain leave to go into the parlour (locutorium) in order to speak. In the cloister they all sat one behind the other: but sideways when talking was allowed... The monk so proclaimed [of violating the vow of silence] had to go out into the center of the chapter and, prostrating, made confession of his fault, and, saying mea culpa and promising amendment, then received penance and rebuke. Should he be accused falsely he could "sweetly" say that he has no recollection of the fault. Special severity was to be shown to the juniors.

ix—She *spoke*. Alas that her first recognizable words were not recorded! No doubt unusual talents were early apparent. The Founder reports being corrected (!) for grammatical innovations with far-reaching metaphysical implications, such as confusing the singular and plural forms, and calling herself "you." From this period dates her discovery that the first-person pronoun, *I*, far from being the plumb line of individuality, was the very thing she had in common with everyone who had ever spoken (making allowances for differences of pronunciation).

THE EXERCISE: Please see OF THE LITURGIES.

x—She *stuttered*.

It is believed that the Founder discovered the power of her so-called "impediment" when, while grieving over a dead bunny, she saw its glazed eye brighten. She kept the justly famous Hopsalot alive for a full twenty-four hours (correctly speaking, twenty-four repetitions of the same hour) by plumbing the susurrous snake pit of the single word *sorry*—a feat of endurance rarely matched—after which she and Hopsalot collapsed together.

A fruit fly taped to the lip of a stutterer will live several hours longer than a fruit fly at large, while a dedicated application of backtalking to a dead fruit fly will revive it for several seconds. Time is measured out in syllables, as Macbeth knew.

THE EXERCISE: Performance by the Alphabet in Absentia.

xi—She *was mocked*. Derided for her stutter by her schoolfellows and scolded by her parents, she taught herself to scan upcoming sentences for words she could not pronounce. Saying "no" when she meant "yes," ordering root beer when she craved sarsaparilla, she lived the negation of a negation, less speaking than not-not-failing-to-speak. All speakers were in this position, she assumed, steering around a great unmentionable, giving voice not to their true desires, but to what little language allowed them. It stood to reason, then, that fulfilment lay at the end of "the path of most resistance," at the stuck, squawking heart of the problem.

THE EXERCISE: The Founder insisted that any child who had not suffered castigation at the hands of peers was insufficiently "tenderized," and would lead the other pupils in a rousing "hullaballoo" of derision, from which the targeted child would emerge pale and weeping. A helper would be waiting with a length of cotton wadding to wrap the child's head until he cried no more even when pinched. The tears, extracted from the wadding by evaporation and condensed in an alembic, were later administered with a dropper as a daily supplement to food, and proved an effective remedy for a recidivist fondness for self.

This routine, it has been agreed, can for the most part be performed internally, with the exercise being completed when the congregant's tears have run down the face and into the mouth.

Self-administered punishment was sometimes frowned upon in the consuetudinaries. From *The English Black Monks of St. Benedict*:

> There are some who practice private acts of mortification and leave unobserved those prescribed by the Rule. Such as these are to be rebuked. Since some of the monks get bled too often and without necessity, in order to get the solatium allowed at those times, it is ordered that bleeding is only allowed once in seven weeks.

xii—She *was silent*.

The Founder spent three years of her young life in silence, broken only by occasional hissing sounds. (It is calumny to assert, as certain older members of the Cheesehill community have done, that she was "scared stiff after her daddy did what he done to her mother"—his guilt was in any case unproved.)

THE EXERCISE: is threefold.

I. *Tongue Sacrifice.*

All participants hold a paper tongue in mouth; the Teeth move through the congregation, snipping off the tips.

II. *The Mouth Theater.*

Before we channel the dead voice, we must silence the living one. This is not the same as simply not speaking. We must practice *unspeaking*. This is the lively production of a silent voice. Paper is the familiar medium for the production of your own voice as a ghost: we practice haunting whenever we write. But our goal at SJVS is to return writing to the mouth.

The Founder designed a number of ways to use paper's natural conductivity to find, tune, focus, and amplify the voices of the dead; as a transitional step to these, which require more time than the Friday service allows, a Miniature Mouth Theater, made of white paper cut square, is held in the mouth for several minutes, and then extracted and viewed.

III. *Shushing.*

Finger to be held to lips for duration of ceremony. Egress into courtyard; celebrants shush everything making a sound: birds, vehicles, telephones, barking dogs, wind, their own clothes; footsteps, speakers, other shushers. Shushers shall, while making sounds with designated parts, shush their head, eyes, mouth, nose, throat, heart, lungs, stomach, gut, anus, vagina, arms, hands, thighs, knees, feet, toes. Church itself to be shushed, Headmistress shushed, etc.

Return to chapel. Prolonged *shhh* to be held through several changes of breath until spittle begins to soak the shush cloth distributed to catch it. Cloths collected to be wrung out, yield added to shush-water stoup.

xiii—She *read.*

Reading takes place in the past—you have to raise the dead to recall where we started. The word *of* sits up, shaking off damp clods and cobwebs; *the* rises in turn, raising a skeletal arm; and *structure* points a juridical finger. Of course, *all* looking is looking into the past, as de Selby has shown, but the special kind of looking that is reading permits a look further back than ordinary looking, without mirrors or telescopes. Thus reading was not just an intimation of her further interest in the dead, but a form of First Contact, albeit unrecognized as such. What, after all, is a ghost? It is an inanimate object or substance—a patch of cold air, a light that comes and goes, a gelatinous blob growing in the basement—that is endowed with some of the properties of intelligent life, but not all. It bears the imprint of the thoughts and desires of someone long gone.

And what is a book?

It is worth adding that the young Founder, chronically out of pocket and thus deprived of chewing gum, had a habit, deprecated by the Cheesehill librarian, of chewing on corners neatly torn off the pages of books. Unquestionably the eating of

Instructions for roving services were not uncommon in consuetudinaries. In the *Rule of Observance of the Most Holy Monastery of Stoudios*, the instructions for Monday morning include the following:

At the second hour of the day when the precentor knocks three times, we assemble in the Church of the great Forerunner… We circle the vineyard close to the monastery with all of us saying in a loud voice the "Christ is risen." Then, we go out in the same manner to the shore of the sea. Having finished an *ektenes*, we go over to the Church of the all-holy Mother of God. Saying an *ektenes* there as well, we turn back to the Church of the Holy Forerunner. Before the entry of the procession, the precentor gives us a signal and the opening prayer is offered… In the same manner, we conduct processions on Palm Sunday and on the Annunciation if atmospheric conditions are clear.

De Selby is a character in Flann O'Brien's novel *The Third Policeman*. Among other theories, he argues:

If a man stands before a mirror and sees in it his reflection, what he sees is not a true reproduction of himself but a picture of himself when he was a younger man… De Selby ever loath to leave well enough alone, insists on reflecting the first reflection in a further mirror and professing to detect minute changes in this second image… What he states to have seen through his glass is astonishing. He claims to have noticed a growing youthfulness in the reflections of his face according as they receded, the most distant of them—too tiny to be visible to the naked eye—being the face of a beardless boy of twelve…

books, full as much as the reading of them, primed her for the passage of spirits.

THE EXERCISE: is threefold.

I. *The Homeopathic Alphabet*.

One of the easiest paper construction projects assigned to students is twenty-six miniature books, one for each letter of the alphabet, with a single page of type comprising one letter. One of these is to be swallowed with water every day, like a vitamin. During the Friday service, however, students are encouraged to down the full twenty-six in succession.

II. *The Wrong Tree*.

Library books to be chewed into spitballs and pressed onto the Wrong Tree.

III. *Brown Wrapper Readings*.

See OF THE READINGS.

> Consuetudinaries paid special attention to the appropriate use and upkeep of spiritual objects. Even the youngest novitiate would only be around for a few decades; an important relic could last for centuries.

xiv—She *wrote*: A simple form of travel in the lands of the dead.

THE EXERCISE: Ink to be sprinkled, see OF THE USE OF SACRAMENTAL INK, etc., as postulants chew pencil erasers or, latterly, wiggle their fingers over an imaginary typewriter. Actual writing is forbidden in the Church.

[xiv (a)—Some satellite schools insert an extraneous Exercise at this point. We wish to repudiate in the very strongest terms the suggestion that the Founder ever performed "sexual intercourse," which is not to say she experienced nothing resembling passion—surely the constant passage of spirits through what we may without stooping to an indiscretion suppose were *all* her orifices, brought the Founder as much pleasure as any merely mortal friction. Adventurous theorists have proposed that sex be seen as a kind of breathing, in and out, in and out, and enthusiasts have even declared it the best possible preparation for Ghost Speaking, in that what one, so to speak, inhales and exhales is only somewhat recognizable as a person, and often makes an eerie noise. The argument has its merits, but clearly "sexual intercourse" and its variants can be foregone, as the experience of the Founder has shown, and many happy lads and lasses have graduated from the SJVS and gone on to successful careers in Ghost Speakership, like myself, without

> Dissent was not tolerated in a consuetudinary. *The English Black Monks of St. Benedict* warns,
>
> > And let the brethren take heed that they fail not in these, for very perilous it is to fail in such laws until they have been revoked by the abbat, or with his permission by the prior or sub-prior in full chapter. There are some who attach little weight to the precepts of chapter, and say: "We will do what is ordered for two or three days, so that we may seem to accept and obey them; but beyond this we don't care." Such as these wickedly sin.

ever, ever—not even once—and in any case sneaking apocryphal and disgusting exercises into the lesson plan under the false aegis of the Founder is nothing short of criminal, and I wonder that the perpetrators do not fear reprisals from Beyond.]

Communication with the dead is one of the hallmarks of medieval monastic Catholicism. The Office of the Dead—made up of psalms, hymns, and blessings—was a formal prayer cycle used for devotion to loved ones who had passed on. Only a few experienced monks were allowed to recite it. The Office was a one-way transmission, and offered no way of knowing whether the message had been received; here, the message travels the other way, from the dead to the living, but it is not clear whether the dead can confirm receipt of it.

xv—She *gave voice* to the dead.

When did it first happen? Was she stomping through the thistles down by the old piano factory (shut down after the incident, and now in ruins), stuttering to herself, as townspeople say she often did, a pale nineteen-year-old with dirty hair and a lucky rabbit foot jumping in her hand? We can only speculate, for she never told us.

THE EXERCISE: After the Board of Dead Fellows has affirmed its attendance via the Salivary and advanced Ghost Speakers among the student body, the Headmistress, behind her screen, will address the congregation, first with the familiar if cryptic words of Clive Matty, then in the voice of the dead Founder, offering advice and instruction.

xvi—She *traveled* down the mouthroad to the Mouthlands. It is a sign of the Founder's very great natural abilities as a thanatomath that she ever returned.

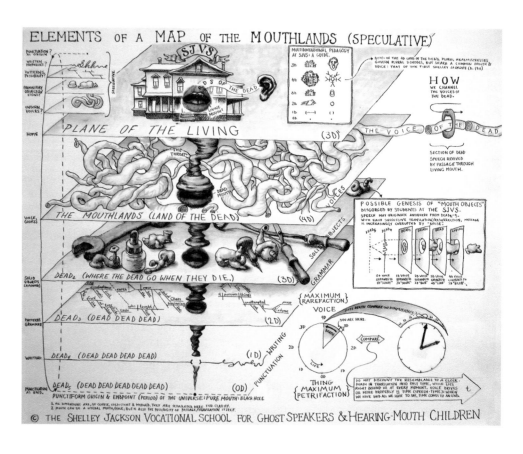

Allegations have spread among the students that she was not the first to take the mouthroad, but sent a senior student by main force onto the path, having earlier tied a thread to his tongue, and obliged him to swallow, the which emerging subsequently at his other end, she pulled vigorously, while bidding him unspeak, thus flipping him inside out. Now, first of all, this method does not work. If you do not believe me, try it—we have all done so at one time or another, despairing of mastering the correct approach. Secondly, the absence of a signature to the Early Dispatches is no evidence of a cover-up—indeed, it lends further support to the supposition that they were drafted by the Founder. Why should she sign what was in essence a "note to self"?

> THE EXERCISE: Brief trip to the Mouthlands. The path is marked on the map at left. (To be performed by advanced students and faculty only.)

xvii—She *emitted mouth objects*, believed to be words in a language of the deader dead, and possibly the building blocks of our own material universe. We leave it to pedants to argue over whether the material of which these objects are made is a solid form of *ectoplasm*, a non-reactive form of *antimatter*, an accretion of dried *mucus*, or some altogether unknown substance. It matters very little.

> THE EXERCISE: Lecture delivered by the silent display of objects held up in sequence by the Headmistress. Congregation may hold up objects of their own to show approval, as for example small pieces of wood, dollar bills, dentures, etc.

xviii—She *died*, after a fashion. The ordinary course of mourning was disrupted by the prompt revival of that familiar voice in the mouth of that senior member of the faculty—now the Headmistress—that she had honored with the task of channeling. The first instructions issued through the new Headmistress were to insert her mortal remains into an oversize manila envelope stamped RETURN TO SENDER. It was delivered to a nearby drop box, and thence, we trust, removed to the Dead Letter Office, as the Founder had desired.

> THE EXERCISE: The congregation to play dead, following the classic sequence: (1) clutch throats, (2) extrude tongues, (3) stare, (4) stagger, and (5) slump. Any child found to be actually

The dead bodies of important church figures, or segments of them, became valued items during the medieval era, and were generally preserved as prized possessions rather than being deposited at the post office. The body of Saint Eligius, a seventh-century bishop, was kept at the monastery in Noyon—it was thought to hold great spiritual importance, and was also an essential revenue source for the chapter.

dead after this exercise will be added to the roster of celebrated former students, and named to the Board of Dead Fellows.

The second part of the exercise is to be performed by the dead; it is the same as that in part i, only backward.

v

OF THE LITURGIES.

—As often as one is moved to do so, a student rises, makes the sign of the zipped lips, and addresses the congregation at a carrying volume with mouth closed. Every attempt must be made to articulate. Listeners to respond to their best guess of the meaning as to an imperative, carrying out whatever they believe they were instructed to do.

—Every six months, the liturgy of mispronounced words, typos, and solecisms, updated weekly, is to be read in full.

—Every Friday, all members of the congregation to recite the Punctatio in its entirety, with the exception of the open parenthesis and close parenthesis, these to be delivered solo by the youngest boy and girl, respectively, among the Hearing-Mouth Children.

vi

OF THE READINGS.

Allowing any book to be used for a reading solves a problem mentioned in some consuetudinaries: the occasional inability of a reader to find the proper volume or passage. *The English Black Monks of St. Benedict* explains that, in the case of readings to be done during mealtimes, "should the reader, however, not be able to find the book at once he recites a short sentence from Scripture (*Deus caritas est*), so as not to keep [the monks] waiting unduly."

Every Friday, a designated reader to select a book at random and cover it with the Brown Wrapper. Any book thus covered becomes the holy book (car-repair manuals, recipe books, scientific texts, etc.); readings to be transcribed and edited into the ever-growing gospels for later study by student acolytes.

Interpreters to draw out the latent meanings of said texts; actions described to be imitated by the congregation.

EXAMPLE 1: "Just to show its versatility, an electric eye took over the role of mouse executioner the other day. It was a rubber mouse, but the effect was the same." *Gloss*: A makeshift executioner destroys an effigy, but the death is real. (The word/rubber mouse is both false and true.)

EXAMPLE 2: "If you are giving a glove-puppet show, it seems to come naturally to speak the words as your glove puppet performs the actions. Because you wear the puppet on your hand, you feel part of it and can identify yourself with the character it is playing. You find you can ad-lib words and persuade the audience to join in." *Gloss*: every human is as a glove puppet to the dead. This is, in fact, what being a self is.

EXAMPLE 3: "It is quite likely that very bad body odors occur about as frequently as extremely pleasant ones." *Gloss*: Speech is a wind produced by a body, and thus may be called a body odor; likewise odors may be considered a kind of speech. The dead speak through us whatever we "say"; thus, insofar as we afford passage to the dead, we are all equally gifted speakers.

At the discretion of the Headmistress, other readings may be introduced.

VII

OF THE USE OF SACRAMENTAL INK, SALIVA, AND CHEWED PAPER.

These may be used at any point during the service when no competing activity is specified.

I—Aspersorium of ink.

The floor to be sprinkled with ink by means of an aspergillum while reciting "Mouth, you have said many things, including this," etc.

II—A single drop of ink.

To be placed with eyedropper on the tongue while reciting, "Whose voice is this with which I ask," etc.

III—Spitballs.

To be chewed and added to the bolus in the antechamber.

IV—Saliva.

The floor to be sprinkled with saliva while reciting, "I am thinking of a word," etc.

V—Eraser crumbs derived from erasing the sacred texts.

May be eaten, or sprinkled on the head.

A wide variety of sacred objects were used in daily Mass celebrations. *The Use of Sarum* calls for a staff, made of wood or precious metal, for use by the Precentor, the lead singer of the monastic choir. Precentor's staffs, also called *baton cantorals* or *cantoral staffs*, were both ceremonial and functional—different staffs might be decorated with precious stones, carvings, or bible verses, but all were used to keep time for the choir, usually by being beaten against the floor.

VIII

OF THE USE OF GAGS, PROSTHETIC MOUTHS, ETC.

For their utility in suppressing the untrained personalities of junior votaries and members of the public, or in opening the throat beyond its natural capacities.

Monasteries used the tools available to them when discipline was required. *The English Black Monks of St. Benedict* describes how, "for very grave crimes," the guilty had to "lie prostrate in the doorway of the church at each hour, so that the monks passed over his body on entering or going out."

I—Gags, Goggles, Earplugs.

Are optional. A nod to the Salivary will bring a junior member with a selection of balks and baffles available for public use. Since the epidemic of 1910, these have been sterilized between uses; on the way out, please deposit your used items in the hamper to the right of the door.

II—Prosthetic Mouths.

To be strapped on over the first. Up to seven may be worn.

III—Filters and Curtains.

Hair, the most important of the parts of the body that are already dead, may be woven into a small curtain for the mouth, a filter for the breath, or both. It is best to use one's own hair, unless deliberately attempting to die someone else's death.

IV—Tongue Depressors, Crutches, Jacks.

To assist in expanding the throat-way.

V—Tongue Corsets, Garters, Reins, Prods, and Forks.

To steer untrained tongues.

VI—Face Diapers.

To be worn only during part V of the service, or, by special dispensation, throughout the service by members of the congregation with uncontrollable logorrhea.

IX

OF SIGNS THAT MAY BE USED
DURING THE OFFICES.

These may be employed at any time the parts required are not otherwise engaged.

I—Zipped lips.

II—Forefingers stuck in one or both ears.

III—Both forefingers wiggling in ears, often followed by:

IV—The cupped ear.

V—Forefinger introduced into the open mouth.

VI— Forefinger drawn across throat.

VII—The raised hand, often held up with the other hand, and accompanied by cries of "Ooh, me"; to be categorically ignored.

VIII—Licking your neighbor's ear; spitting into their mouth.

IX—Weeping, striking oneself in the face, tearing at eyes or mouth with fingernails, etc.

X

OF THE SERVICES THAT THE PUPILS SHALL RENDER TO THE COMMUNITY.

I—Of Ectoplasm.

The School shall provide sufficient ectoplasm to prime the throats of the young girls of Cheesehill for the ghosts of adolescence, viz, a "punchard" per child per week, and additional vials for Visiting Hour, enough for both the parents of prospective students and for inquisitive neighbors, and at funerals a quart, unless it be that of a student, and then it shall provide two quarts.

Item: in consequence of the scandal of 1903, in which a student prank resulted in widespread reportage that SJVS ectoplasm was nothing but egg whites, let any ectoplasm suspected of falseness be returned to the Headmistress for testing.

II—Of Olykoeks, or "Dough-Nuts."

On every Friday those members of the Cheesehill community who attend the service will receive an olykoek with a hole through the center to represent the mouth, zero, death, the wind that blows through us. Colorful "jimmies" on top will signify that although our life centers around the void, we may take time to savor the details of our material existence. Into each perforated olykoek or "Dough-Nut" the cook or koek will introduce a skein of ectoplasm.

III—Of Gags.

The School shall provide haircloth and balsa-wood gags for all Cheesehill community members who wish to silence themselves or others.

Item: these shall be *clean* and free of tooth marks.

IV—Of Boluses.

The School shall masticate any book (exclusive of its binding) supplied by members of the Cheesehill community without regard

Writing on *The Use of Sarum* in an 1881 issue of *The Wiltshire Archæological and Natural History Magazine*, Canon W. H. Jones observed:

> There is indeed one characteristic of the Consuetudinary, which, though perhaps subordinate to its main purpose, can hardly fail to strike anyone who attentively studies it—the way, that is, in which it assigns to each member of the cathedral body, not only his own distinct office, but also his own personal share in the work and services of the cathedral. It regards all of them—from the bishop down to the youngest acolyte—as forming one compact religious household; and the individualism of the separate members is merged in the corporate life and work of the whole.

In his introduction to the St. Swithun consuetudinary, G. W. Kitchin writes,

> It is interesting to note in passing, that at the time of the Napoleonic Wars salt was so dear in England, that in some parts of the country clergymen's daughters... went round the table after dinner with a knife and piece of paper, scraping off the salt that was left on the plates, and afterward carrying it down as a welcome gift to the cottages in the village.

for content, and shall return to the members a bolus or spitball from any designated page or, if unspecified, a page of the chewer's choice, of no less than one half inch in diameter, to be delivered moist.

V—Of Translation Services.

Being that all material objects may be words in a language of the deader dead, the students offer their help to all members of the Cheesehill community, free of charge, in translating into plain English puzzling objects around the home, viz, knobs of hair extracted from drains, bezoars, unidentifiable utensils, etc.

XI.

OF THE MANNER IN WHICH A DEAD PUPIL SHALL BE SENT INTO THE MOUTHLANDS.

Along with daily life, consuetudinaries did have to address the treatment of the dying. *The English Black Monks of St. Benedict* explains:

> When it was announced that a brother was dying, the whole convent gathered together in the church, together with the abbat, and then went in procession to visit the sick… The public confession is made by the sick man himself if possible, and he is absolved by all his brethren… And now the sick man prepares himself for death by resuming the old ascetic practices. No longer does he take meat (unless he recovers), nor does he use a softer bed than usual.

We have all seen it: sometimes a student dies during exercises. It may be because of congenital frailty or some other "natural" cause. It may be that the program was simply too rigorous for him, or that with praiseworthy enthusiasm but lamentable results he experimented with techniques beyond his capabilities. Did he get lost down his own throat, practice nonbreathing techniques without a spotter, get himself in a choke hold, inadvertently utter a kill word? Perhaps duty called him to serve a higher function as a student representative to the Board of Dead Fellows. Or perhaps he merely wished to deceive the Salivary into thinking so. The cause of death must be determined before any course of action can be decided upon. This is done by asking him; the dead do not lie. The answer, of course, will not come directly from the corpse, except under the most unusual circumstances, but will be delivered via one of our talented Hearing-Mouth Children.

After death, according to the *The English Black Monks of St. Benedict*,

> The deceased, clad in his night garments (it was specified that the clothes had to be good, even new), with his face covered with a *sudarium*, was borne into the church, and there the office of the dead was sung, and vigil kept around the body, which was never left until the funeral. He was borne to the grave by his brethren, and laid therein by two monks vested in albs.

Regardless of the cause of death, the child (even the wicked, deceitful child) must be returned to the Vocabulary with appropriate pomp. A cork is to be inserted into his throat, and the mouth carefully filled with ink. A quill pen is to be dipped in it, then employed to write the child's name upon a piece of blank paper. The pen having been returned to the mouth, the paper is to be folded into an airplane, and shown to the congregation, who are to respond by writing their own names on their own pieces of paper. Matches are handed round.

Three hundred blazing paper planes in full flight make, you may be sure, a very pretty picture.

Illustrations by Shelley Jackson.

GATE

a new pantoum by Troy Jollimore

Though everything on me had been scanned and cleared—
I had been preapproved—still, I felt somehow impure.
A seraph with a clipboard sang, Hurry up and wait.
I wondered which memories they would let me keep.

I had been preapproved. Still, I felt somehow impure,
like meat or milk gone bad. We longed for ascension.
I wondered which memories they would let me keep:
I had not thought debt had undone so many,

like meat or milk gone bad. We longed for ascension,
for grace, freshly aware of our burdensome weight.
(I had not thought debt had undone so many.)
We watched for the opening of the blessed gate,

for grace, freshly aware of our burdensome weight.
(Though everything on me had been scanned and cleared.)
We watched for the opening of the blessed gate.
A seraph with a clipboard sang, Hurry up and wait.

DIRECT

a new pantoum by Joel Brouwer

Would you maybe like some ice cream?
Are you in pain? Does history exist
As an objective reality
Or as a set of interpretations

In pain? Does history exist?
Do you recognize anyone
In this set of interpretations?
Or in this picture?

Do you recognize anyone?
Do you like the darkness and light
Of this picture?
Did your loved ones get burned up?

Do you prefer the light on or off
When your women menstruate?
Do you burn the bodies of your loved ones
Or participate in other rituals?

Do you allow your women to menstruate?
Have you eaten your feces
Or participated in other rituals
To evade or escape your enemies?

Have you eaten? Are your feces
Important to your belief system
Or merely a form of evasion or escape?
Would you say a kind of vacation?

Is your belief system important
To you or your superiors? Do you believe
This is a kind of vacation
Or that anyone is superior to you

Or to your superiors or that you know
The name of that large bird
That one circling right above you?
Do you know it's been driving us crazy

Wondering about the name of that large bird?
Ice cream or feces: Which do you prefer?
Do you know it's been driving us crazy
Wondering who you might recognize in pictures

And whether you'll choose ice cream or feces?
Did anyone in this picture burn up
In wonder and recognition and might?
Or become or fail to become superior?

Was this picture burned in the dark?
Have you noticed you are in the picture
And we your superiors are becoming
Crazier and burning in pain and love?

Have you noticed we are in the picture
Burning to love you in the dark
And crazy with pain for you to love us
And wondering whether this too shall pass?

Darkness, will you burn or love us?
Or maybe some ice cream?
Or for the wonderful to pass
As an objective reality?

CRACKPOT ARCTIC OCTOPUS

a new pantoum by Nicky Beer

I want to show you my blueprints.
This is where I'm going to put up the pistons,
The silver horses. I've been dreaming of
Building a giant carousel underwater, you see.

This is where I'm going. To put up the pistons
Close by the sea-vents—risky, I know, but—
Building a giant carousel underwater! You see
Why it must be done. I try to keep calm,

Close by. The sea vents risk. I know but
Fucking and fighting in a green haze.
Why? It must be done. I try to keep clams
Quiet by drilling holes in their heads.

Fucking and fighting in a green haze
Will drive anyone quite crazy after a while.
Quite. By drilling holes in their heads,
The Eskimos released their demons into the sky.

Will drives anyone quite crazy. After a while
Down in the seabed it all became so clear to me.
The Eskimos released their demons. Into the sky?
Nonsense. They seeped into the ice,

Down in the seabed. It all came to me. So be clear—
This is not really what I wanted,
The nonsense they seeped into the ice,
Though I've made an amusement of it all the same.

This is not real: what I wanted,

The silver horses I've been dreaming of,

Though I've made an amusement of it. All the same,

I want to show you my blueprints.

THE MOST NATURAL THING IN THE WORLD

a new pantoum by Walker Pfost

It's the most natural thing in the world,
killing a man. Before you
know it, you've done in about seventy.
You get strange habits, like

killing a man before you
eat breakfast, or just whenever you see one
who's got strange habits. Like
a disease, the desire spreads from when you

eat breakfast to just—whenever. You see? One
can't be too careful, then. Your friends get
the disease, the desire, spread from when you
killed one of them, and they think they

can't be too careful—your friends get
knives and ropes to come after you for
killing one of them. And they think (they,
your friends) why not kill their friends, who get

knives and ropes, too. Coming after you (for
blood now boils like oil, or sunlight),
your friends (who survive their friends) believe
each time will end it all.

Blood now boils like oil, or sunlight.
Know it, you've done in about seventy
each. Time will end it all.
It's the most natural thing in the world.

CONTRIBUTORS

NICKY BEER's first book of poems, *The Diminishing House*, will be published by Carnegie Mellon University Press in early 2010.

JOHN BRANDON's novel *Arkansas* was published by McSweeney's in 2008. His short work has appeared in the *Mississippi Review*, *Words & Images*, the *Believer*, the *Duck & Herring Co.*, and *Subtropics*. He is looking for a teaching job.

JOEL BROUWER's most recent book of poems is *And So*. He teaches at the University of Alabama.

DOUGLAS COUPLAND is a writer and artist who lives in Vancouver. He is currently finishing a biography of Marshall McLuhan. His next novel, *Generation A*, will be published this fall.

JENNIFER MICHAEL HECHT has written two books of poetry and three books of philosophy. She teaches in the graduate program at the New School in New York City.

SHELLEY JACKSON is the author of the novel *Half Life*, the short story collection *The Melancholy of Anatomy*, and several children's books. In 2004 she launched her project *SKIN*, a story published in tattoos on the skins of 2,095 volunteers.

BEN JAHN's fiction has appeared in *ZYZZYVA*, the *Greensboro Review*, *McSweeney's*, and *Torpedo*, and is forthcoming in the *Santa Monica Review*.

TROY JOLLIMORE's first book, *Tom Thomson in Purgatory*, won the 2006 National Book Critics Circle Award for poetry. A chapbook of new material, *The Solipsist*, was published in 2008.

DAN LIEBERT is a stand-up comedian, and writes the "Dan Liebert, Verbal Cartoonist" feature for mcsweeneys.net. He lives in a small town on the Ohio River.

BYRON LU is a first-year medical student in Philadelphia.

MARY MILLER's stories have been published in the *Oxford American*, *Black Clock*, *New Stories from the South 2008*, and elsewhere. Her story collection, *Big World*, was published in February.

DOUGLAS W. MILLIKEN's recent essays have appeared in *Salt*, *Ghoti*, and the OmniArt anthology *Mourning Sickness*. He spends a lot of time in Portland, Maine.

WALKER PFOST went to school at Furman University, and now lives in South Korea.

WILL SHEFF is the singer and songwriter for the rock-and-roll band Okkervil River. Their most recent album, *The Stand Ins*, was released last fall on Jagjaguwar. He currently lives in Brooklyn.

CHRIS SPURR lives in Kent, England. He teaches art at a secondary school.

BILL TARLIN grew up in Framingham, Massachusetts, hitchhiked to Chicago in 1981, and was a student editor of the first issue of the *Columbia Poetry Review*. He now administers clumsyyogi.com.

DAVID THOMSON has been writing about the movies for forty years. His books include *The Biographical Dictionary of Film* and *"Have You Seen...?": A Personal Introduction to 1,000 Films*, as well as several novels. His memoir, *Try to Tell the Story*, was published earlier this year. He lives in San Francisco.

TONY TRIGILIO's most recent publication is the chapbook *With the Memory, Which Is Enormous*. He directs the creative writing—poetry program at Columbia College Chicago, and coedits the journal *Court Green*.

JOY WILLIAMS is the author of nine books, including, most recently, the short story collection *Honored Guest*.

WORKS REFERENCED

PANTOUM

Hikayat Hang Tuah. c. 1800.

Tom Hood. *The Rhymester: Or, The Rules of Rhyme: A Guide to English Versification. With a Dictionary of Rhymes, an Examination of Classical Measures, and Comments Upon Burlesque, Comic Verse and Songwriting*. D. Appleton and Co., 1911.

William Marsden. *A Grammar of the Malayan Language*. Cox and Bayles, 1812.

Thomas John Newbold. *Political and Statistical Account of the British Settlements in the Straits of Malacca, Viz: Pinang, Malacca, and Singapore*. John Murray, 1839.

Gleeson White. *Ballades and Rondeaus, Chants Royal, Sestinas, Villanelles, &c: Selected, with Chapter on the Various Forms*. D. Appleton and Co., 1901.

WHORE DIALOGUE

Nicolas Chorier. *L'oeuvre de Nicolas Chorier*. Bibliothèque des Curieux, 1910.

Bradford K. Mudge. *When Flesh Becomes Word: An Anthology of Early Eighteenth-Century Libertine Literature*. Oxford University Press, 2004.

LEGENDARY SAGA

"The Fornaldar Sögur Corpus." Translated by Gavin Chappell, Samuel Laing, and Peter Tunstall. *Northvegr*. www.northvegr.org/translation/fornaldar.php.

The Heimskringla, or the Sagas of the Norse Kings: from the Icelandic of Snorri Sturlason. Translated by Samuel Laing. John C. Nimmo, 1889.

The Story of the Volsungs. Translated by William Morris and Eirikr Magnusson. Walter Scott Press, 1888.

Snorri Sturlason. *Kongesagaer*. J. M. Stenersen & Co., 1900.

Snorri Sturlason. *The Prose Edda*. Translated by Arthur Gilchrist Brodeur. Oxford University Press, 1916.

NIVOLA

Miguel De Unamuno. *Obras Completas*. Afrodisio Aguado, 1958.

Miguel De Unamuno. *Niebla*. Translated by Warner Fite. H. Fertig, 1973.

BIJI

Duan Chengshi. *Chinese Chronicles of the Strange: The "Nuogao Ji."* Translated by Carrie Reed. Peter Lang Publishing, 2001.

Carrie Reed. *A Tang Miscellany: An Introduction to* Youyang zazu. Peter Lang Publishing, 2003.

Leo Tak-hung Chan. *The Discourse on Foxes and Ghosts: Ji Yun and Eighteenth-Century Literati Storytelling*. The Chinese University Press, 1998.

John Minford, Joseph S. M. Lau. *Classical Chinese Literature: An Anthology of Translations*. The Chinese University Press, 2000.

SENRYŪ

Yamaji Kanko. *Kosenryū meiku sen*. Chikuma Shobō, 1998.

Haruo Shirane. *Early Modern Japanese Literature: An Anthology, 1600–1900*. Translated by James Brandon. Columbia University Press, 2002.

Jessica Milner Davis. *Understanding Humor in Japan*. Wayne State University Press, 2006.

Light Verse from the Floating World: An Anthology of Premodern Japanese Senryū. Translated by Makoto Ueda. Columbia University Press, 1999.

R. H. Blyth. *Senryū; Japanese Satirical Verses*. Greenwood Press, 1971.

SOCRATIC DIALOGUE

Cicero. "De Inventione." *The Orations of Marcus Tullius Cicero*. Translated by Charles Duke Yonge. George Bell & Sons, 1888.

Oscar Wilde. "The Decay of Lying." *Intentions*. T. B. Mosher, 1904.

Plato. *Apologia*. Translated by D. F. Nevill. F. E. Robinson & Co., 1901.

Plato. *De Republica*. Translated by Allan David Bloom. Oxford University Press, 1900.

Plato. *Ion*. Translated by Benjamin Jowett. Internet Classics Archive. http://classics.mit.edu/Plato/ion.html.

Plato. *Rempvblicam*. Oxford University Press, 2003.

Xenophon. *Symposium*. Translated by H. G. Dakyns. Project Gutenberg, 2008.

Francis Hodgson Burnett. *The Lost Prince*. The Century Co., 1915.

"Buying a Ticket to Graustark." *The Literary Digest*: November 17, 1928.

Anthony Hope. *The Prisoner of Zenda: Being the History of Three Months in the Life of an English Gentleman*. Henry Holt & Co., 1894.

Anthony Hope. *Rupert of Hentzau*. Henry Holt & Co., 1898.

George Barr McCutcheon. *Beverly of Graustark*. Dodd, Mead and Company, 1904.

George Barr McCutcheon. *East of the Setting Sun*. Dodd, Mead and Company, 1924.

George Barr McCutcheon. *Graustark: The Story of a Love Behind a Throne*. The Lakeside Press, 1901.

George Barr McCutcheon. *The Prince of Graustark*. Dodd, Mead and Company, 1914.

George Barr McCutcheon. *Truxton King*. Dodd, Mead and Company, 1909.

Vladimir Nabokov. *Pale Fire*. Putnam, 1962.

Billy Reed. Quoted in *Kentucky Bluegrass Country*, by R. Gerald Alvey. University Press of Mississippi, 1992.

Robert Louis Stevenson. *Prince Otto: A Romance*. Roberts Brothers, 1886.

CONSUETUDINARY

A Consuetudinary of the Fourteenth Century for the Refectory of the House of St. Swithun in Winchester. Edited by G. W. Kitchin. D. D. Warren and Son Printers and Publishers, 1886.

Canon W. H. Jones. "On the Consuetudinary of S. Osmund." *The Wiltshire Archæological and Natural History Magazine*, volume XIX. Alan Sutton Publishing, 1881.

R. B. Pugh, Elizabeth Crittall. "The Cathedral of Salisbury: From the Foundation to the Fifteenth Century." *A History of the County of Wiltshire*, vol. 3, pp. 156–183. 1956.

Ethelred Luke Taunton. *The English Black Monks of St. Benedict: A Sketch of Their History from the Coming of St. Augustine to the Present Day*. John C. Nimmo, 1898.

The Use of Sarum. Edited by Walter Howard Frere. Cambridge University Press, 1898.

Customary of the Benedictine Monasteries of Saint Augustine, Canterbury, and Saint Peter, Westminster. Edited by Edward Maunde Thompson. Henry Bradshaw Society, 1904.

NEXT ISSUE

stories from the year 2024,
by Sheila Heti, Jim Shepard, Salvador Plascencia,
Heidi Julavits, Chris Adrian, and others.

TO SUBSCRIBE

—store.mcsweeneys.net—